ABOUT THE AUTHOR

Following the success of *House for all Seasons* (#5 bestselling debut novel in 2013), Jenn wrote three more stories for Simon & Schuster AU before the UK's Head of Zeus published her fifth full-length novel —*A Place to Remember*. Known for both her signature small-town stories and her nomadic life with Myrtle the Turtle (a purple and white caravan), Jenn established Wild Myrtle Press while travelling somewhere between North Queensland and NSW, later joining forces with Pilyara Press—a diverse group of women writers and creatives who helped her publish book #6. The follow-up to her Calingarry Crossing Collection, *House of Wishes* gained national recognition in 2020, awarded second place in the Romance Writers of Australia Book of the Year Awards.

   Country Crush is a collection of BIG little stories, again with a backdrop of contemporary country life. *Enjoy!*

JENN'S OTHER TITLES
House for all Seasons
Simmering Season
Season of Shadow and Light
The Other Side of the Season
A Place to Remember
House of Wishes

www.jennjmcleod.com

PRAISE FOR JENN'S NOVELS

HOUSE FOR ALL SEASONS (A Calingarry Crossing novel)
'The author has created a living, breathing small town, peopled with wonderful people—an amazing achievement.' *Greg Barron, author*

SIMMERING SEASON (A Calingarry Crossing novel)
'The characters are so well fleshed out that you fall in love with them all. A story full of country feels and community spirit.' *Veronica, Goodreads*

SEASON OF SHADOW AND LIGHT
'Stunning writing, spellbinding storytelling, art in all its glory and the message that it's never too late to make things right.' *Bookgirl, Beauty and Lace Book Club*

THE OTHER SIDE OF THE SEASON
'Jenn's writing is evocative, gorgeously descriptive and transports you to the places she writes about. The twists were fantastic and though there were some that you could see coming, there were others that sucker-punched you out of the blue.' *Michelle, Beauty and Lace Book Club*

A PLACE TO REMEMBER
'I read *The Thorn Birds* forty years ago and still remember it. Similarly, I think the emotion and poignancy of this story will stay with me too.' *Jane Hunt (UK)*

HOUSE OF WISHES (A Calingarry Crossing novel)
'One of the most beautiful books I've had the privilege of reading. The way the characters blend and intertwine, leaving the reader with every emotion possible and closing the book with tears and love, is masterful.' *Patricia, Goodreads*

Compact stories for country lovers

Country Crush

Jenn J. McLeod

In collaboration with Pilyara Press

Published as an anthology in Australia in 2021 by Wild Myrtle Press: a collaborative project with Pilyara Press.

National Library of Australia Cataloguing-in-Publication entry

Author: McLeod, Jenn J., author.

Title: Country Crush/Jenn J. McLeod.

ISBN: 978-0-6485708-4-4 (paperback - ten short stories)

ebook editions (five stories in each): That Time in Tanglewood (ISBN: 978-0-6485708-5-1) and One Friday in Sunflower ISBN: 978-0-6485708-6-8)

Subjects: Australia–Fiction. Short stories, Australian. Anthologies.

Dewey Number: A823.01

Cover design: Wild Myrtle Press

Image: www.storitella.com.au, @stori.tella (Insta) @storitella (Facebook)

Wild Myrtle Press and Pilyara Press do not mass produce books. We use Print On Demand (POD) publishing because POD books represent economically viable management of the world's forests, are environmentally responsible and socially beneficial.

Printed and bound in Australia.

That Time in Tanglewood

'I have never known any distress that an hour's reading did not relieve.'

— MONTESQUIEU

THE TIMEKEEPER'S STORE

It is exactly 11:11 am. I know this because clocks surround me.

Like my father, I am the town's watchmaker, and between us we have kept timepieces in the small town of Tanglewood ticking for over one hundred years. I am also a watcher of people, although confess to mostly observing Millicent York from my workroom in the front corner of the jewellery store. Same day, same time, she walks by my store window; such is the stately lady's routine nowadays. While Tanglewood's shopping precinct and main street is expansive and tree-lined, there is no missing her. Not even among the Saturday morning cafe crowd outside Miss Pink's Patisserie. I dare say, should the town's entire population of six thousand crowd the cracked footpaths to bursting, the stylish and self-assured Millicent York would stand out by a country mile.

Today, when she walks by my store, something about her appearance has me fearing the worst.

Is Millicent York dying? Death *is* only a matter of time. Of this I am desperately aware after mastering my craft for over fifty years. The thing about being an old watchmaker, however, is time too easily becomes the overriding focus. And yet, I can't replace the broken cogs of a life any more than I can stop them from wearing down, prevent time draining memories away, or reverse the clock hands that count down a person's existence on this planet. All I can do is set the watch before handing the timepiece over. What happens next is up to the owner.

U

11:59 am, same day …

I'm surprised and delighted when Millicent turns into my store, her hands clutching the patent leather handbag ordinarily reserved for Sunday best. I'm aware of this because she attends church each week, arriving early to secure the same seat: on the aisle, one row in front of me but on the left-hand side. Her bag, tucked tight at her feet, matches the black pumps poking out from under beige cotton trousers. Her hat—small and stylish—covers silky white hair, but I see only the dreamy young girl who used to occupy herself by collecting confetti remainders from the Bible-rests on the back of the pew.

One Sunday, she'd scooped the pile of colourful dots into a cupped hand and poked the paper pieces on her palm into patterns. Then, one by one, the dots had disappeared. By the time the minister had finished preaching trust and faith and everlasting love, and the congregation closed their hymn books, the confetti pieces—much to her mother's chagrin—littered Millicent's blonde crown of curls.

Later that year, proud parents had packed the same church pews as bright-eyed teenagers were matched by height, then paired. I'd already stuffed my shoes with cardboard to appear taller, and not a single person had been aware of my ruse as I walked down the carpeted aisle beside Milly Brown, vowing it wouldn't be the last time.

Ten years later, I witnessed Milly walking the same aisle as a bride. She was resplendent in white and marrying my best friend, Toby York. Two years after that, I was a bystander at the christening of baby Brian, and a second son twenty-four months later. All such happy events, until the 11th day of the 11th month, 2011, when at precisely 11:11 am, church bells tolled for Toby York, the town's lovable larrikin. I remember the time because that's the moment I witnessed a tiny piece of Millicent York die.

'Millicent! Great to see you.' I replace the jeweller's loupe that normally occupies one eye with a pair of pince-nez and shuffle out from behind the glass partition separating my workroom from the store. With each step, my frame straightens and I grow taller—no cardboard required—until finally I am face-to-face with the woman I've always admired and loved.

'Good morning, Angus.' She returns my smile.

'And to you, Milly. That sunshine looks nice.'

'Why, yes, it is.' She replies as if the weather no longer makes a difference to Millicent's days.

By rote, I've unrolled a length of black cloth over the glass counter and rested clasped hands at its centre, as if giving thanks. I suspect I am this morning. 'Can I show you something in particular?'

'Actually, Angus,' Millicent places her handbag on the glass cabinet with a cache of glistening watches beneath. 'I have something to offer you.' She unclips the tortoiseshell latch on the purse and draws out a small pouch which she promptly upturns. The contents cascade over the black display cloth and twinkle like stars against the night sky.

'My, my, what have we here?'

'I'm hoping you can melt the gold and refashion the diamonds and sapphires into something a little more modern.'

I'm quick to assess the colour and the clarity in the larger stones on offer. One—instantly recognisable—makes me hesitate. 'You can't possibly mean all these pieces. Such memories.'

She barely looks at the glittering conglomeration. 'I have no need to save trinkets from the past. Our memories are the only precious jewels we should concern ourselves with, Angus. And they are in here.' She touches a hand to the side of her head, 'And in here'. The same hand moves to that place on her chest where a heart ticks over, like the hands of a clock. 'It's time,' she says, her words almost a whisper. 'Time to tidy my life and make a move. A new house requires many changes.'

'A new house?' This is news the town grapevine has bypassed.

'Yes, and I'm afraid decluttering becomes a necessity when one downsizes,' she explains.

'But these pieces, Millicent ... They are special.'

'And my granddaughter is soon to be engaged—so Tanglewood's grapevine tells me. Before long I suspect my grandson will do the same.' Millicent pulls something from the inside pocket of her handbag. Her photograph, frayed at the corners, is faded; not so the pride in her eyes. 'Both children are much older now, of course. They live very busy lives,' she adds, as if noticing the quizzical knotting of my brow. It's because the picture is tired looking; as is Millicent suddenly. 'Oh dear, you are very polite to let an old woman carry on.'

As she smiles, I am a teenager again, eager for a moment with sweet Milly Brown. 'I've always enjoyed your ramblings,' I say. 'I'm also interested to learn all I can about my customers when I am to design something unique to them.'

'For my grandchildren,' she corrects while sliding the prized photograph—clearly more precious than any jewellery item—safely back in her bag. 'Assuming you'll have sufficient to make two rings? One for each grandchild?'

I assure her the gold and gemstones are plentiful and suggest we talk design.

Waving her hand, Millicent pooh poohs the idea. 'I've no clue about such things. Might your sons, or your grandchildren, be more in touch with what today's youth are wearing? You have so many young people in your life, Angus.'

'I do, yes.' I visualise Heatherbrae House with its long hallways and busy walls of framed family photographs. I recall how Mary had insisted I hang multiple pictures of every family gathering so she'd feel surrounded by love and happy memories when she finally slipped away.

'I wish I had more up-to-date photos. I often ask,' Millicent adds, somewhat defensive, as she moves to the next display case containing dress jewellery. 'But in this day and age of digital this and that, well ...' She drops her gaze, pride siphoning the early signs of her tears as she searches the display case. 'I think nothing too showy for my grand-daughter. She's quite refined and stylish, so I'm told.'

'Then I suspect she takes after you,' I say, watching a red glow, visible under the light dusting of face powder, invade Millicent's cheeks. She is again radiant.

If only I could control time, I'd pause my life here and now; long enough to appreciate the effort Millicent York puts into her appearance: setting hair that frames her face and applying makeup to a complexion requiring no such enhancement.

'It's hot under all these lights,' I say, noting her glistening top lip. 'Let me get you a chair.'

'I'm fine, Angus, thank you. Please, about the jewellery design ...'

'Yes, yes, down to business,' I say, professional mask back in place. 'Perhaps your grandchildren would like input? Ask them next time they visit. They *do* visit regularly?'

'I see Tim, but he is busy on the family property with his parents. Tabitha returns to Tanglewood periodically, but you know children?' she says with a tentative smile. 'And my sons are both working hard, having taken over the farm. They work such long hours and the grandchildren enjoy busy social lives. Not even the festive season remains sacred.'

'Is that why I didn't see you in church last Christmas?' I ask.

'Mmm, yes, I was in a terrible dither over the family lunch. For the first time in years we were to spend the day at my house in town. All of us together, Tim and Tabitha included. I was so excited and there was so much to prepare until ...' Millicent's tone saddens as she explains the call she'd received from Brian on Christmas Eve. Something had come up. The family cancelled Christmas. Not one visit on the day. Millicent straightens her frame and lightens her voice.

'The old saying is true; your daughter is your daughter for the rest of your life, while your son is a son until he takes a wife.' She shrugs and smiles a fusion of joy and sadness. 'Trust me to have two boys.'

Me too, I might have said while glancing at my sons' framed faces hanging on the shop wall.

Instead, I smile. 'Well, Millicent, if you're certain you want to give all these up—this one in particular.' The setting is solid, the stone significant, the design stylish and carefully crafted. A fine piece of work it is today and a fine piece when I made it forty years ago. 'A fine, fine specimen,' I say aloud.

'And as you are aware, Angus, the gentleman who gave it to me on our first anniversary was also a fine specimen.' We smile in memory of Toby until Millicent says, 'I see no sense in hanging onto something that makes me sad.'

'Very well.' Having tried as much as I dare, I reach under the counter for a velvet-lined box befitting the collection. 'What if I was to bring a few design sketches to the bowling club next week?'

'Oh, I'm afraid bingo is no longer possible. The move has me situated out of town, too far from Tanglewood.'

Both surprise and disappointment render me mute. A single syllable is all I can manage. 'Oh?'

'Yes, with Brian changing things on the farm and Nathan shifting into the house in town, the family considers Sunflower Retirement Village more suited to my needs.'

'I'm sure they do.' I remark. 'When my sons casually left a brochure on the kitchen table five years ago, after Mary died, I set them straight. I told them "I'm not dead yet".'

I hold off sharing the rest of the conversation—that such places aren't a home, and a sprinkling of picture frames in a small, single-bed room cannot disguise the basic, easy-clean cocoons designed for people nearing their use-by date. I won't be spending whatever time I have left in God's waiting room; not if it means leaving behind the community I've been part of all my life. I'm about to express my concerns when Millicent smiles. Suddenly, the effect of halogen lighting on polished gold and silver is no match for the sparkle in her eyes. There is so much life in the deep, chocolate brown irises staring back, but I bite my tongue and mind my business. This is not the time.

'I'd best be off,' she says. 'Thank you for caring, my friend.'

Two weeks later …

Again, I am staggered by the dullness of the halogen-lit jewellery display as I espy Millicent's face through the store window.

'Your timing is perfect, Milly!' My shuffle from the workroom is unusually sprightly. 'Please, sit down.' I drag a stool to the counter and hold it steady while she perches on the edge, her handbag clasped on her knees.

'You are so kind, Angus. That walk from the bus stop is not easy.'

'You're catching a bus from the retirement village? Is Toby's old pride and joy with the mechanic? I know Jock's always wanted to get under her hood; they no longer make classic cars like yours.'

'Ha! That damn car will no doubt outlive us all,' she quips, her smile stilling, fading, gone. 'The thing is, my son insisted I stop driving and, rather than have the car sit in the garage, his wife arranged transfer of ownership to young Tim.'

I'm saddened by Milly's news. My sons have been less than gracious about the York boys—and their wives. Just last Tuesday, during our weekly catch-up dinner, they'd disparaged the Yorks for fighting over the family estate and this disturbs but does not surprise me. Jewellers bear witness not only to life's most joyous unions, we can come face-to-face with the rejected, abandoned, or forgotten. I've helped wives and mothers, their spirits broken as badly as their hearts, convert jewellery to cash to buy a ticket to freedom; perhaps to find real love while there's still time.

Millicent York's enemy is not time, and time is not stealing her life away piece by precious piece. Her children are. Not content to take their mother's home and treasures, they have taken away her independence, her confidence and, now, her car.

Two more weeks pass …

Millicent drops by, and when I offer to show her the work-in-progress, she declines. 'I'd prefer to wait for the finished item.'

When something in her eyes suggests she misses the joy of life's little surprises, I make a silent promise to be present the day she collects the completed rings so I can witness her delight.

Another fortnight passes …

Delight is not what I see on Millicent's face as she passes by the shop on the arm of a well dressed, middle-aged woman I'm aware is Brian York's social-climber wife. Millicent barely manages a glance in my direction before she's hustled across the road towards the bank that occupies the shop next to Miss Pink's Patisserie. Milly's expression is one of disappointment, of regret and longing, of sorrow and hopelessness.

And fear.

Greed—and not hers—is sucking the life out of Millicent York.

It's that time …

Even before glancing from my work to the array of wall clocks, I know it's time. I grab my jacket, leave Son #1 with the shop, and cross the street towards Miss Pink's.

When Milly invites me to join her for profiteroles, I explain my self-imposed prohibition of Miss Pink's pastries. Then, when I sit and order a serving, she laughs.

By the time morning tea is over, I'm dizzy from both the sugary, soft-centred choux pastry and from Millicent York; with her sweet laugh my new addiction, I can't get enough. Part as we must, I suggest driving to bingo together. I am, of course, prepared for every objection: *Yes, Sunflower is a distance to drive. Yes, I'll be travelling in the dark.* Instead, she tilts her head to the side and says, 'It's a date.'

And we make the arrangement a regular one, our bingo table at the bowling club complete once more.

The time is 11:11 exactly …

Millicent is resplendent in red—the twinset a match to her loafers, and the string of pearls a match to her silvery locks. Gone are the customary grey trousers and sky-blue shirts. Her hair is newly set, and the smell of fresh lacquer pervades my nostrils. We arrive at our regular café table the exact same time and I jiggle my Windsor knot and visualise the nervous schoolboy about to take his first communion—the one so desperate to partner the girl he planned to marry he'd crammed his feet into shoes stuffed with height-enhancing cardboard.

Five decades later, we have time on our side. We are two cogs in a watch, perfectly tuned, the wheels still turning, still measuring the passage of time. Today we are on a date; we've had many. No customers to interrupt us, no busy bingo table to contend with. Just two people sharing a single serve of Miss Pink's profiteroles.

The trembling in my hands as I lift the lid on both boxes is not from the sugary treat, but from the finished jewellery designs.

'Oh my!' It takes her a moment before she reaches almost reverently to caress the remodelled memories. 'Everything old really can be new again,' she chimes, examining both rings. 'You and your boys are wonderful, Angus. These are marvellously modern.'

'My youngest son deserves all the credit for the design,' I confess. 'And my eldest brought them to life. But I've also been busy, Milly—with this.'

As I lift the napkin covering the concealed package on the table, then peel back the chunky lid, there is a heart-stopping pause.

'Don't think me presumptuous,' I say, somewhat ruefully. 'I wanted you to have something, too, Milly.'

Her brow creases, eyes narrowed, confused. 'You're giving me a new watch? Why?'

'Firstly, it's not new.' I scoot the display box towards her for a closer look and Milly's mouth curls into a grin.

Then she laughs that laugh I love. 'So, this gift of yours is an *old* watch, Angus?'

'Dear Milly,' I say, cautiously. 'This is the timepiece from your cache, but remodelled.'

Her eyes widen. 'That ancient thing?! But this is too beautiful. How, Angus?'

My cheeks tingle with a blush as I explain. 'I used leftover gold for the case and embedded the remaining diamond chips in the bezel—here, around the outside. Give me your hand, Milly.' I slip the watch onto her small wrist, the band a perfect fit. 'I thought you should keep something.'

When she doesn't look up straightaway, I picture tears filling her eyes. But no. She's lifted her face to mine, her smile growing. 'It's keeping time, Angus! The hands ... They're ticking over. And here's me thinking it was only good for scrap.'

'Old doesn't mean disposable or useless, Milly,' I tell her. 'A little love and attention can give life to so many things, even an old timepiece.'

'It was so reliable until,' she pauses. 'Until five years ago when it stopped at ...' She falls silent.

'At 11:11, Milly. I remember.' I reach out my hand and grasp hers. 'Things break, my dear friend, or we lose a precious piece. There are so many parts to a life. Even more to a watch, and with the intricacy and complexity such, that if one were to remove a part—big or small —the device would cease to function. You and I both understand this in the context of life. But, Milly, most can be mended. Some take more time than others and something, like a watch, can end up different, but not any less beautiful, or meaningful, or useful.

'No watch—no watchmaker—can turn back time, Milly, but as you see ...' I position the face with its ring of diamonds under the ray of sun striping our sidewalk table. 'It is possible to repair and reshape our memories. We can look at something that's always been there, but with fresh eyes and a new appreciation.'

'You've been such a big part of my life, Angus.' When she squeezes my hand, I am twelve years old again, ready to walk that church aisle. 'You helped make my memories. You still do.' She drifts to another place momentarily as if gathering her thoughts. When she looks into my eyes, she says, 'Time has got away from us, hasn't it, Angus?'

I shake my head and shrug. 'Time is neither calendar nor clock, Milly. Time is a gift—one we can't control but can stop controlling us.'

She sighs. 'When did we get so old, Angus?'

'Young? Old? These are words, Milly. With a little remodelling, you and I can be marvellously modern.'

We laugh together, and over a second profiterole she looks across the table and tells me, 'We have time, Angus. Shall we make the most of it together?'

I smile, nod, breathe. I agree. 'We do indeed have time, Milly.'

⌣

'Time brings all things to pass,' said Aeschylus. But I know this because I know about time. Clocks surround me. I am the town's watchmaker, and like my father before me I keep timepieces in our small town ticking over. I am also a watcher of people, although these days I confess to mostly observing Millicent York from where I sit across from her at the breakfast table in the little Heatherbrae House we now share, here in Tanglewood.

SEW SPECIAL

I'm about to tell you a tale, dear friends, about life and love and joy. It's the story I've told many times before—the one about our Audrey's fortieth; the day she met her flyboy.

Her instructions that day had been clear.

'I'm serious! No cake with forty candles, no corny cards, no cacophonous chorus of Happy Birthday.'

Audrey insisted the only thing she needed was more customers for her little alterations business, because a hem here, a tuck there, and the steady hum of an overlocker put takings in the till and food on the table.

During the forties and fifties, the back workroom of her grandmother's shop had been Audrey's playground, where she and her sister, Judith, grew up with the drone of sewing machines and the susurration of satins, tulle and taffeta. Brides-to-be, bedizened with the promise of a happy ever after, would emerge from behind change-room curtains so Grandma Fortuna could add jewels and lace trim, pinch waistbands, and fuss with cleavages. Every bride transformed into a princess, each with her own special prince.

The sixties had brought broken promises and sadness to our Audrey, until a decade later, while spending her fortieth birthday in that same workroom, everything changed.

'Are you going somewhere, sis?' Judith asked.

'Well, let me see,' Audrey said while tightening the white laces on the patent, knee-high granny boots. Her reply? That of a devoted, but exasperated, older sister. 'I'm leaving you—my trusty business partner —with our best friend, Mai-Lee, to mind the shop while I make a delivery.' She smirked, switched off the work light above her sewing station, and secured the black ponytail of hair with two twists of a satin scrunchie. Swinging the macramé bag over one shoulder, Audrey settled a red beret to the side of her head and finger-combed the fringe of her bob cut. 'I assume you don't have a problem with me leaving?'

'What kind of delivery?' Judith persisted. 'And how long will you be gone?'

Audrey slumped, her huff a frustrated one. 'I'm not sure how long. What's with the interrogation, Jude? I told you last week. I'm delivering those reams of fabric for Saturday's church fete. We'll never use them.'

Judith rose from her work stool as if pricked by a thousand sewing pins. 'But you can't.'

Audrey's part confused, part amused expression was not an unusual response when dealing with her sister. 'Can't what? Give away excess material to the local church? It's the seventies, Jude, and a good twenty years since Marilyn Monroe made shocking-pink satin a girl's best friend. Something has to go; the storeroom's bursting at the seams. At least help me cart them to the car.'

'I don't mean the fabric can't go,' Judith told her. 'I mean *you* can't.'

With each bemused blink, Audrey's mascara-laden eyelashes and fringe tangled. 'Can't what, Jude? I don't understand.'

'You can't go anywhere. Not today. Not yet.'

'Why not?' Audrey checked the modish digital wristwatch. 'It's already past 11 am. Half the working day is over.'

'Well, exactly!' Judith slapped her thigh. 'We need our morning cuppa. I'll pop the kettle on before you go.'

Audrey eyed her sister. 'What are you up to, Jude? Out with it.'

'All right, all right, you got me,' Judith sighed. 'You didn't want a fuss, but we had to have a cake.' Judith nodded towards the front counter. 'Mai-Lee's about to light the candles. Ahem! Isn't that right, Mai-Lee?'

Audrey groaned. 'Didn't I say no cake, no forty candles, and no gifts?'

'Yes, but by then the cake was already ordered—with your name on it—from the bakery next door. Good news, though,' Judith beamed. 'There are only ten candles. We couldn't fit all forty.'

'You are hilarious, Jude! There'd better be no presents.'

Judith blushed. 'All depends what you mean by "present", sis. To me, unless it's wrapped—and Mai-Lee and I haven't wrapped a thing —then it's not officially a gift. Unless surprises count as gifts …' The flash of Judith's open palm silenced Audrey. 'And by surprises, sis, I simply mean we plan on filling your day with fun things and treats, like a surprise cake.'

'I saw your wink, Judith,' Audrey said. 'If you two have something silly lined up I will—.'

'Relax, sis, today will be perfect. I promise.'

'Perfect?' Suspicion was sprinkled through Audrey's voice, and for good reason. One previous so-called perfect present from her sister had been a bikini wax gift voucher. The so-called beauty procedure was catching on with the singles crowd and, according to Judith, 'an occasional spruce-up down-under' was not only considered acceptable, it might make Audrey feel better about getting back in the saddle after the not-so-perfect present from her horrid, hippy husband a few years earlier. The man's sorry-it's-not-working-out-so-I'm-leaving note had shocked everyone at the time.

After the breakup, it was Sew Special—the small alterations business specialising in tricky repair jobs no one else wanted—that had kept Audrey's life from falling apart at the seams. Judith helped, with the odd gift and occasional sisterly lecture urging Audrey to put as much effort into mending her life as she did into mending the customers' clothes.

'There's no ripping my heart out and whacking it under my trusty Husqvarna,' Audrey had once responded. 'Mending a torn heart isn't like putting a patch on a pair of pants.'

Audrey looked ready to launch into another lecture about the perfect gift for her fortieth being happy customers, then home for dinner, a wine and a good book, when the tiny brass bell over the shop's doorway rang out.

'*Ooh la la!*' Judith mumbled behind a hand. 'Now that's what I call the perfect addition to a special day. I'll let you serve this customer, sis. You can thank me later.'

Clean-shaven and wearing a dark suit with epaulettes and insignia on broad shoulders, the uniformed man whipped away his aviator sunglasses. He eyed the dwindling birthday candles with the rainbow of dripping wax obliterating the pink *Happy Birthday Audrey* message and said, 'Looks like I'm in the right place, even if my timing is off.' He glanced at his watch. 'It's only 11:11. I can grab a coffee and come back later.'

'No, your timing's absolutely perfect. My sister will look after you.' Judith's gentle shoulder shove nudged Audrey, forcing her to trip closer to the counter.

'Absolutely perfect?' Audrey mumbled as she eyed the gentleman on the other side of the counter.

His impeccable presentation was possibly making him more dashing than he might otherwise be, but a man in a uniform was rare in a small town where, to most Tanglewood locals, dressing up meant dusting off the stockman's hat and donning a chequered shirt, chaps and a pair of weather-beaten boots. Something was askew about this morning's first customer—other than the pilot cap perched on a mop of brown hair. Audrey suspected the answer was in the giggle-fest going on in the back corner of the workroom.

'What's so funny, you two? Mai-Lee?' she asked. 'This had better not be …' Audrey's shoulders sagged. 'Oh, good grief! Please, tell me you didn't waste your money on another fad, Jude.' Arms crossed, she glared at her sister from the front counter. 'You did, didn't you? This guy—Flyboy—is one of those new-fangled strippergrams we were giggling over in last month's *Cosmopolitan*.' Judith had laughed herself silly, while Audrey could think of nothing worse. Even the magazine had described the latest hen's night craze as 'the show everyone gets a kick out of except the bride-to-be'.

'Jude, I hope you can get a refund, because this is not my idea of the perfect birthday gift. Okay?' Audrey turned to address the man directly. 'My apologies. Sisters!' She shrugged another apology. Having a sibling ten years her junior, and enduring a plethora of childish pranks as kids, she was accustomed to Judith playing jokes— her sole purpose being to embarrass—while denying every action.

With Judith rendered mute, and Flyboy's bewildered expression suggesting the same, someone—Audrey—needed to say something, or else surrender to the cake, the cards, the chorus and, now, the cute guy and his strippergram act.

'Fine!' Audrey gushed and huffed, keen to get the birthday surprise over with so she could get on with her work. 'I'm ready. Go ahead.' She'd approach this latest so-called-perfect present in the same way she'd faced the bikini wax the previous year—intrepidly. 'Take it away, Flyboy. I've got a million things to do. As for you two …' She turned towards the workroom and wiggled a finger. 'Both of you get over here and enjoy the show. You've paid for it.' Audrey made a point of tiptoeing to peer over the counter. 'And he does have a nice butt. Does Flyboy come with a ripcord we grab in the event of an emergency?'

'No parachute today,' Flyboy, straight-faced, replied. 'Perhaps I should just take off my jacket?'

'Works for me,' Audrey said, charting a flight path over the tall, toned frame as she strutted seductively to the customer-side of the counter. Leaning back, arms and ankles crossed she smiled and tipped her head. 'Do you need music? I could hum a few bars of "Come Fly With Me", or maybe "Fly Me To The Moon", maybe let me play among your—'

'Audrey, no, stop, please!' Judith had found her voice, but her feet stayed glued to the old floorboards at the back of the work area, her face flushed red, her eyes and mouth agape.

Flyboy, however, remained nonplussed as he examined the graffiti-like icing. 'I take it the birthday cake melting under those candles is yours? Audrey, is it?'

'As if you didn't know my name already,' she retorted. 'Or is this where I use the line "I can be whatever, or whoever, you want me to be, Flyboy"?' Audrey was enjoying herself way too much. 'Do I call you something other than Flyboy?'

'I'm Buck.'

A jolt of amusement straightened Audrey's spine. 'Buck! Is that right?'

'My father's choice,' he explained. 'I was an airforce brat, born in the States before we moved to Australia. According to my old man, my birth coincided with the airing of the first Buck Rogers radio program.'

'As in Buck Rogers Space Ranger?'

'Yep! Buck Roger Spencer at your service.' He doffed his cap, his smile the kind to melt hearts—and candles.

'I guess that makes you destined to fly, one way or another,' Audrey said. 'I, on the other hand, always wanted to be Wonder Woman with an invisible aeroplane and my Golden Lasso of Truth that's capable of forcing those who tangle with it to obey.' Audrey reached out to his chest, her index finger giving the tie a quick flick. 'Don't say I didn't warn you, Flyboy.'

'Noted,' he said, his laugh melding with Audrey's. 'Now, about my jacket …?'

'Ah, yes, about that!' Audrey looked at the garment he'd draped over the counter. 'I had expected you'd take it off with a little more, ah, pizzazz.' She ran a finger over the lapel before taking in the detail on his shirt, including the embroidered wing insignia on his shoulders. 'Whilst I'm sorry to say I'd rate your performance so far as lacklustre, my compliments to whoever put your outfit together. It's a fine job, Captain. Very authentic.'

'As authentic as this?'

Audrey squinted at the ID he slipped from the breast pocket of his shirt. As she read aloud, 'Trans Australia Airlines,' all cockiness disappeared, her gaze darting between the badge, her sister, and the customer with the growing grin. 'You mean ...? But, I thought ... Aren't you ...?'

'Sis, I tried to tell you.' Judith said,

'Clearly not hard enough,' Audrey rejoined while slinking behind the counter. 'I'm so sorry for the misunderstanding, sir. I thought ... I had the impression—'

Flyboy laughed. 'Don't worry about it. I'm flattered. No one has ever mistaken me for a strippergram before today. By the way, thanks for the nice butt remark. You're so special.'

The words snapped Audrey to attention. 'I beg your pardon?'

He pointed to the Sew Special shop sign in the window. 'The name of your shop. I do have the right place, don't I? Sew Special?'

For the third time in as many minutes, Audrey groaned an apology and tried putting on her professional mask; not easy to do with her foot constantly in her mouth.

'The woman at the airport kiosk suggested you,' he explained. 'I needed my uniform fixed in a hurry and she said you and your shop were one of a kind and exactly what I needed. Right now, I'm asking myself if maybe she was right.' The pilot retrieved something from the pocket of his jacket on the counter. 'But I'm captaining a return flight to Sydney later today and time is ticking—'

'Of course, yes, sorry. I'll start straightaway and have your coat fixed up in no time.'

'While you're doing that, would you please replace this in the lining?'

Audrey inspected the ornament in his outstretched palm—a Hand of Fate talisman, a small red stone at its centre. Years before, her grandmother's shop had sold similar charms and trinkets.

Granny Fortuna, named after the Roman goddess of fate, had dabbled in all things mystical while she single-handedly raised Audrey and Judith in the two-bedroom house behind their alterations shop squeezed between the town barber and the bakery.

Fortuna had sewn her last seam the day she died, leaving behind a business that combined haute couture with her love of everything mystical. As a result, the odd, compact dress shop had once been littered with good luck amulets, gemstones, and incense.

Audrey had, reluctantly, found new homes for Fortuna's treasures, bauble by bauble. Only the heart-shaped pewter dish remained on the counter, filled with so-called lucky gems—stones her grandmother had claimed encouraged positive energy and success in business.

Audrey looked from the pewter dish, to the lucky metal charm in Flyboy's hand, and back to his face.

'Let me get this straight,' she said. 'You want me to sew this metal talisman back into the torn lining of your pocket before I stitch up the hole the talisman's sharp metal points probably created in the first place?'

'That's correct.' He sounded pleased. 'This one's been sewn into the lining of every uniform I've worn for the last twenty years.'

'But, why?' Audrey asked. 'I don't understand.'

'Well,' Flyboy began, 'I was in the region doing my flight training when there was an incident on the last day and a forced landing on the outskirts of Tanglewood. I believe this talisman saved my life.'

'This old thing? How?' A lover of good storytelling, Audrey leaned forwards to rest her elbows on the counter and cupped her chin in her hands.

'Well, we'd completed our training, you see, and I was due to fly the crew back. My first flight as Captain,' he told Audrey. 'The day before, I headed into town for a bit of a spruce-up and was putting my jacket back on after a haircut when it snagged on the barber's chair. Ripped the pocket clear off. Lucky for me there was a little clothing alteration place right next to the barbershop and … Wait a minute!' Flyboy's storytelling stalled as he took in the street visible from Sew Special's expansive window. Various footpath signs urged passers-by to stop. The bakery boasted fresh Easter buns, while the adjacent hair salon was offering a free blow-wave with every henna colour. His attention returned to the counter where he prodded the little pewter dish. 'This could be the same shop. Fancy that! My first day in a new role, as Flight Training Manager at the regional base, and here I am again. How amazing!'

Audrey agreed. 'Amazing is one word.'

'Even more fascinating is what happened when I returned that day to collect the repair job,' Flyboy continued with an added air of excitement to his narration. 'That's when the crazy old lady explained why she'd stitched a lucky charm with a garnet into the lining. Symbolically, the stone ensures safe, speedy homecomings while helping people find their destiny. The woman was quite a character.' He chuckled. 'Memories of the encounter, and her, stayed with me for years. Almost as long as the sandalwood that had permeated my jacket during its short sojourn in the shop.' A smirk lifted one eyebrow. 'Not a smell fully appreciated by colleagues in a compact cockpit on a three-hour flight. I think the old lady's name was—'

'Fortuna,' Audrey muttered, the whispered memory barely audible.

'Fortunate indeed,' he mistakenly agreed. 'First flight and first emergency landing later the same day. No mechanical cause identified, no explanation, and, miraculously, not one injury.' He stopped to nudge the talisman on the counter. 'I've been convinced ever since about the garnet. Meeting that crazy old lady was the luckiest and best thing that could have happened to me.'

Flyboy pulled his Cary Grant face—a cheeky smile, starting as two tiny twitches at the corners of his mouth, before launching into a grin that overwhelmed his face.

'Luckiest until today maybe,' he said in a low voice.

'Actually,' Audrey blushed. 'I said it was Fortun-*ah*—my grandmother. When she died, I took over this business with my sister, Judith.' Audrey turned towards the workroom where a speechless and mortified Judith could only shrug and smile. 'She may be needing a lucky charm of her own later today.'

'Oh dear!' Flyboy grimaced. 'I'm sorry about your grandmother and sorrier still for calling her crazy and old in the one sentence. I jumped to the wrong conclusion and that's not very admirable.'

'Let's call it even, shall we?' Audrey said, happy to move on as there was nothing admirable about misleading a customer. Fortuna's talismans were not real and the garnet he was so attached to was nothing more than a glass bead. 'Fortuna probably was a little crazy,' she added. 'Although, I'm sure that statement seems like a case of the pot calling the kettle black. And I suspect you're also questioning why you came into this crazy little shop for a second time.'

Flyboy grinned. 'To have my jacket fixed.'

'Oh, yes.' Audrey's words trickled out on a laugh while she struggled to position the jacket on a coat hanger and ask if he'd prefer to wait for her to do the job. 'It won't take me long.'

'I have a few things to do before my flight,' he replied. 'Besides, returning might mean enjoying a repeat performance.'

'Oh, ah, no, I …' Audrey pressed a palm to her chest and peered up from under eyelashes heavy with Mary Quant mascara. 'If it's all right with you, I'd like to stick with a more professional greeting when we next meet.'

The corners of Flyboy's mouth did the Cary Grant thing again—twitching twice before he chuckled. 'Either way, Audrey, I'll look forward to that meeting very much.'

U

I love listening to Mai-Lee narrating our story. Even now, as one trembling leg after the other moves me towards the altar, and with age slowly and cruelly taunting me by playing with the memories, Flyboy's parting words in the shop on my fortieth birthday remain as strong as ever.

I'll look forward to that meeting very much.

How I will live without him is beyond the limits of my understanding. There isn't one second out of the 86,400 each day when I don't hear those words and picture Flyboy in our little shop all those years ago. It is 1973, and he's young again, the handsome and charming Flyboy in the crisp white shirt, epaulettes on broad shoulders and a Cary Grant smile.

Forty years later the memory of his smile still buffets me with such force I wonder if I will breathe again. All I can do is place the palm of my hand against my chest and wait; four fingers curling into a fist so tight around my talisman pendant I can feel my nails pressing faint half-moons into the thinning flesh of my palm. With my head lowered to let the surge of tears recede, the only sound is the roar of sad silence.

Tanglewood's chapel is full of teary faces, all staring at me, waiting for me, expecting me to fall apart at the seams. But I remain stoic, pray my eighty-year-old legs do not betray me, and glide precautionary hands over the solid wood of the pulpit for support. It is old, like me, and etched with as many stories from the past.

One look at my family in the front row and I am energised with the power of their extraordinary love. My grown-up twins sit with their own children, arms outstretched to welcome a teary Mai-Lee back to her rightful place in the family pew. Settled and relaxed now her narration is over and she's no longer the centre of attention, Mai-Lee looks at me from the spot where Judith, my adorable, reckless, best friend of a sister would have sat had cancer not taken her away. How I've missed her crazy birthday gifts.

As the family fusses over Mai-Lee, offering tissues and solace after the moving tribute, I must dig deep for the last skerrick of courage, draw strength from the love in the room, and respond.

'Thank you, Mai-Lee, my dearest friend. Thank you for a lifetime of friendship and for filling that place in my heart, of a sister lost so long ago and far too soon. Thank you, too, for your splendid story-telling and for shining light and laughter on what is the saddest occasion. Having met in laughter, it seems fitting that you help me say goodbye in laughter. And, oh, how Flyboy and I have laughed these past forty years, especially at your joie de vivre each time you tell this birthday story.' I pause, my voice rattling with regret as the persistent sob, determined to free itself from deep inside my throat, finally escapes. 'But it seems my handsome Flyboy, the hero in your story, has taken his final flight without me.'

As I look around the church I ask myself: how is it possible to feel so loved by so many, yet feel so lost? Then, finger by finger, I unclench the fist pressed over my heart and release the stranglehold on the small pendant—Flyboy's gift for our fortieth wedding anniversary, just passed. Mounted in fine gold, the year 2013 engraved on the back, and with a real garnet in place of glass, it's the same Hand of Fate talisman my grandmother, Fortuna, had sewn into his jacket all those years ago; the same one that brought us together; the same one that had blessed my Flyboy with safe homecomings all the years since.

As it is time for my final words to the assemblage of family and friends, I draw a breath and scan the packed chapel.

'Please do not weep for me, dear friends, for one thing is certain. The tiny talisman from Mai-Lee's story will now protect me until it's my time to see my Flyboy again.'

I fix tear-filled eyes on the framed photograph at the altar and his words come to me: *I look forward to that meeting very much.*

ABOUT MIDNIGHT

'So, Ben Ledson, what time do you call this? And you have a dog!' Although dazzled by the porch light, Claudia's sense of smell was working fine. 'Why? You know I hate dogs.'

Two big brown eyes (the dog's, not Ben's) stared back at her.

'You don't hate dogs, Claud.' The way he spoke was reminiscent of her late father: gentle, perceptive, indulgent. 'You have a sad memory attached to them. We both do.'

She still refused to look at the animal, her voice firm. 'Yeah, well, the mutt stays outside.'

'But, Claud—'

'No buts, Ben Ledson. No slobbering dog on my polished floors.'

'But—'

'Do you realise the time?' Claudia did. After the doorbell had startled her awake, she'd looked at her phone and cursed the hours: 11:11 pm. 'Well, do you?'

'About midnight, or thereabouts?' Ben replied. 'Please, Claud, it's important.'

Too tired to protest, she gave him the full trifecta—the eyeroll, the sigh, the shrug—then unlatched the security screen door. As she flicked on interior lights and tiptoed in bed socks down the narrow passageway, a big, black burst of energy barrelled past her, almost tripping Claudia as it struggled to find purchase on the timber board and came to an unceremonious stop in the neat-as-a-pin living room. All black, except for the greying muzzle, the old dog sat up and shook its head, a suspended string of slobber stretching to the floor.

'Great!' Claudia stepped around the hairy interloper (the dog, not Ben) to top up the kettle from the kitchen tap. 'When you didn't show, I packed your meal away in the freezer. Sorry, Ben. I can do coffee or tea?'

'Water's fine.'

'For you, or for your furry friend?' Claudia reached deep into the cupboard under the sink and felt the familiar bone-shaped bowl.

Her mood immediately darkened as she rinsed dust from the decorative dish, before filling it and grabbing a tumbler for Ben. But when she turned around with his water, Ben's toothy grin and bright eyes made her smile. She'd always loved her best friend. Claudia had known him as long as she had Jack, and yet it was always Ben—the best mate—who'd brought out 'the Claud cackle', as he called her embarrassing Woody-Woodpecker-meets-Porky-Pig laugh. Not that there'd been much laughter of late. This past year had been more difficult, with people in town avoiding her because they had no words. Never Ben. He'd been there for her with words of wisdom and advice from their first meeting; they'd shared a connection ever since. They'd shared Jack. They both missed him still. Ben more so, as the twenty-nine-year-old mates had been friends since school.

Every day, Ben and Jack had ridden their bikes as far as the multitude of motley remote mailboxes on the main road where they'd wait for the school bus. Then, on the ten kilometres into town, they would invent new pranks to terrorise the teachers and tease the girls at Tanglewood Primary School. Like the time they'd deposited a blue tongue lizard in the change room on sports day. As they matured, the games changed, and when girls—eager to impress—teased the boys back, Ben became the duo's straight man. As recently as eighteen months ago, when adventurer Jack arrived back in town in time for the annual country dance, Ben's quick-witted, unassuming sidekick act had provided the perfect icebreaker.

Claudia couldn't know at the time how important Ben's playful banter would be to her in the months ahead, doing the impossible, letting her forget, helping her move on.

'*E-ewe!* Look at the mess, Ben.' Over-enthusiastic lapping by the unwanted interloper (the dog, not Ben) had created a water bowl tsunami. 'This. Isn't. Funny.' Cursing while yanking multiple sheets of paper towel from the roll, she soaked up the slobber, fully expecting a typical Ben quip. But tonight he wore his super-serious face; the one Claudia knew well, the one he'd worn the day of Jack's funeral. 'Are you going to sit down, Ben, or at least tell me what this is about?'

'Do you recognise him, Claud?' He nodded at the dog while shaking the backpack off his shoulders, tossing the bag next to the blackened fireplace in the corner.

'Which bit in particular?' Claudia looked at the smelly ball of black tangles now semi-reclined, a back leg frantically scratching a freckled stomach, tongue flopping about and teeth bared in a kind of ecstatic snarl. 'And do we need to see *that?*' She screwed up her face and pointed to the dog's maleness.

'Hey!' Ben chuckled for the first time since arriving and nudged the animal into a sit. 'Put it away, you bloody skite.'

Claudia was part way through a mental shopping list—flea bomb, room deodorant, disinfectant—when she noticed the animal's muddied chest blaze—a patch of hair, normally white and almost the shape of an arrow tip. Such a mark reminded her of a superhero emblem, and superheroes always reminded her of …

'No!' But within a heartbeat, she knew. She looked from Midnight to Ben's face and back again, remembering the beloved mutt outside her bedroom at sunrise each morning.

'Captain Midnight and I are off to save the world,' Jack would call from where he jogged on the spot on her teeny square of front lawn, while the well groomed dog chased its fluffy tail in excited circles. 'Out of bed, lazybones.'

Despite her vehement refusal to join him, Joker Jack soon turned the daily wake-up ritual into a game. He'd wait until he was passing her house—shirtless, biceps bulging—to do his warm-up exercises. Claudia would play along by drawing back the curtains and tempting him to skip his run. But, no matter how raunchy the pose, Jack never took the bait. Claudia soon learned nothing—not even her offer of morning sex—could disrupt Jack's fanatical fitness regime. Staying healthy for the next adrenaline-charged adventure was what Jack Diamond lived for: skydiving, canyoning, crocodile wrangling. He'd done crazy stuff all over the world before returning to Tanglewood. When Claudia had asked him why he took risks, he'd smiled and said, 'No pressure, no Diamond.'

Once warmed up, the game over, Jack's short, sharp whistle would lift Midnight's nose from the latest hole in the garden bed. Tail and tongue wagging madly, the dog would bound down the street ahead of his master, leading the way to the walking track above the gorge.

Initially amusing, his energy addictive, Claudia soon learned Jack was all about Jack, which made people mould themselves around the popular guy in town—Claudia reluctantly. During their six months together—perhaps the word *together* was not an appropriate word with Jack—she'd twice contemplated breaking up, but something always stopped her. It was fear—although she never knew if she was afraid of losing Jack (the boyfriend) or Ben (the best mate).

At that moment, with her thoughts lost in the big, brown eyes staring back (the dog's, not Ben's) Claudia was afraid of losing her composure.

'No, it can't be,' she said, her words a whisper. 'It's Midnight?'

Ben nodded and breathed a loud sigh, most likely relieved she hadn't burst into tears. From the day they'd met, Claudia had cried a lot of tears over Jack, while Ben had been the one to mop them. Even without his mate, Ben remained the friend she could talk to about anything. Well, almost anything. They never discussed her relationship with Jack when he'd been alive, and even with him gone these past twelve months any *Jack* conversations remained guarded.

'Just got back from picking him up from the Fuller's Creek pound,' Ben said. 'He's not looking quite himself.'

'Him and me both.' Claudia twisted the chaotic tangle of her own black tresses into a knot and, without regard for the drool puddle, kneeled down, dusted off the white patch of the dog's chest into the palm of one hand and stroked the familiar triangular shape with the other. When she looked up at Ben, she hoped she was smiling. 'Fuller's Creek is three towns away and twelve months is a long time to be lost.'

'Yes, it is, Claud. Way too long for anyone.' Ben dropped to his haunches to wrap an arm around her shoulder, squeezing tight.

He was comforting Claudia the way he'd done at Jack's funeral, despite his own grief on the day. For weeks afterwards, anytime sadness and regret threatened to consume her, he'd find ways to console her, not knowing there was guilt in the mix. If Claudia had gone jogging with Jack she would've been there. She might have talked him out of risking his life for a dumb dingo. The day she'd mentioned her guilt to Ben, he'd remind her. Nothing ever stopped the larger-than-life Jack Diamond, who considered everything doable, including scaling barehanded down a cliff face to save a stranded animal.

Behind the beguiling and oh-so-bed-worthy man she met at Tanglewood's single's dance, was a sensitive bloke who loved saving lost souls and collecting strays. Even though she let herself fall a little, Claudia knew Jack would never be *the one*. Wild guys like him looked for flings, not forever-afters. There was also no halfway with Jack. You either kept up or let go, and such ultimatums didn't sit well with a cautious Claudia. So, while Jack did what Jack loved, Claudia's weekends turned into waiting games, and she passed the time with Jack's long-suffering best friend. Sometimes she and Ben cooked or went driving. Once he took her fishing, claiming it was the most relaxing sport in the world.

'Unless you're the worm,' Claudia had disputed.

On rainy days they would watch DVD movies on her big-screen TV, always with fingers crossed that the adrenaline junkie would come home safe. How sad and ironic something as mundane as his routine morning jog and a needy dog had stopped Jack.

Police had found a howling Midnight first and the dog never left his master's side until the rescue crew winched Jack's lifeless and broken body out of the gorge. As the helicopter took off, so did the injured dingo, with Midnight in pursuit. He never came home, leaving Ben without his two best mates. That same day, Claudia decided to hate dogs.

With another squeeze of her shoulders Ben said, 'The place has been bloody quiet since Jack. It'll be good to have Midnight back in the house for company.'

Claudia almost knocked Ben off his haunches as she stood and walked back to the kitchen sink. 'What have *I* been all this time, hmm? Chopped liver?' she called to him, sounding snappier than intended. 'Besides, you've barely been at your place this past year. You've been here almost twenty-four-seven.'

'You needed me,' he said somewhat defensively. 'Didn't you?'

Claudia backed down, took a breath, smiled. 'We needed each other, Ben.'

I still need you, Claud!

Ben wasn't brave enough to say the words aloud for fear of breaking the thin thread connecting the pair. Without Jack to bind the trio, Ben feared the smallest amount of tension might send Claudia back to the city, and he couldn't let her go. *Not yet!* There was so much to say but, as usual with Claudia, the words in his head were not equal to the task because Ben wasn't Jack, even though as lads he'd emulated his best mate, trying to keep up, trying to score with the girls. Ben eventually grew up and stopped competing, satisfied there was merit in being the Robin to Jack's Batman.

Until Claudia.

Ben ruffled the hair on the dog's head. Maybe finding Midnight was a sign. The dog had disappeared the day of Jack's accident, despite the lost dog flyers he and Claudia had posted around Tanglewood and neighbouring towns, like Sunflower. Originally Ben's dog, after discovering the abandoned puppy in a sack on the side of the road, the puppy bonded with Jack. It had been much the same in school when Ben, the dutiful sidekick, had settled for his mate's cast-offs. At the time, Ben had been cool with his wingman role, until the local dance when the best mates had spotted Claudia and her peroxided girlfriend gyrating and giggling in time with the DJ's choice of disco classics.

Keeping with the conventions of Bachelor and Spinster Balls of old, blokes attending a country dance these days rarely made the dance floor. Most stayed glued to the bar area where they sucked on cans of Dutch courage while ogling the single ladies from a safe distance. But Ben had known Claudia was the one for him the second she laughed and tossed her hair. Like a schoolboy, Ben had quickly put dibs on the black-haired beauty, aware Jack was more the blonde-babe type.

The score, however, became clear well before last drinks, and although not the first occasion Ben had lost a girl to the dynamic Jack, this one had mattered, the defeat devastating him. To make the situation even more frustrating, earlier that evening Jack had joked with the blokes at the bar about preferring a risky base jump off Kilimanjaro over committing to a serious relationship. Three months was his limit.

Until Claudia.

At home later that night, having invented an excuse to leave the function early, Ben had wondered if Claudia might actually be the one to rope Jack, finally taking him out of circulation and giving the other blokes in town a chance. Little did Ben know, six months from that dance, as the sun chin-lifted over the horizon, Jack would be no more and Ben would never again have to vie for a woman with his best mate, and for more reasons than one.

As it turned out, Jack wasn't into girls. According to his mum who'd confided in Ben after the funeral, asking him to keep the revelation information to himself, she'd been waiting—hoping—her son would figure things out for himself and find happiness with 'a nice young fellow'.

Despite the news, whether out of loyalty to Jack and his mother, or cowardice on Ben's part, he kept up his friend-only status with Claudia as her sidekick. He could at least be on hand when she needed him, or until she was ready for someone else in her life: someone Ben hoped would be him despite being less adventurous and not as amazing as Jack.

Ben was, in fact, far from reckless; a good thing, too, given his vocation. A mining engineer with a reputation for risk-taking had slim job prospects. Desk-bound and cautious, he didn't dive in without thinking, nor deal in maybes. Engineers don't build first and test later. They don't tempt fate or make decisions before understanding the outcomes of a project. So, with no way of predicting or controlling the outcome should Ben reveal his feelings to Claudia, he refrained. Better still, he developed a project; a step-by-step approach. So far, he'd successfully worked through steps A–G. But tonight ... Tonight was, like, somewhere around 'U', 'V' or even 'W'. This was not the time to put their friendship's foundation to the test. Tonight was about Midnight.

Ben always believed the dog would find his way home; that he'd only run because he'd been frightened and confused over Jack's unresponsiveness and the helicopter's roar as it lifted off with his master. Midnight simply lost his way.

Twelve months later, after a National Park Ranger two hundred kilometres away uploaded a picture on Facebook, Ben posted the comment: *He's mine.* And he was, like he should have been from the start. Only one other thing Jack had taken as his own required remedying; one person Ben wished could be his.

'Claudia?' he blurted. 'There's something I need to—?'

'Phew, Ben!' Claudia groaned and fanned her face.

'Hey, no it wasn't me,' he quickly established, although not quite the confession he'd had in mind. 'Bloody hell, Midnight!'

Dragging the smelly beast by the scruff, Ben realised he might have ruined his relationship with Claudia if not for the smelly interruption. What was he thinking? With his emotions in overdrive, he'd romanticised Midnight's homecoming and made the dog out to be a sign when he wasn't.

'You're not,' he told the dog. 'You're a fleabag in need of a poop and a bath.'

Ben found Claudia at the kitchen sink when he returned with Midnight.

'I'd better not step in any surprises tomorrow,' she said.

'Relax, Claud, he only piddled.'

She flashed an open palm. 'Spare me the details.'

'Okay,' Ben said, happy to leave out how Midnight's post-piddle pawing of the ground had accidently uprooted clumps of the decorative Mondo grass she'd nursed through the Tanglewood's recent water restrictions.

'When you said you'd be over tonight with big news, Ben, I imagined champagne in flutes, not water in a bowl. Is finding Midnight your big news?'

'Ah, no, not exactly.' Ben's mouth was so dry at that moment he could have wrestled Midnight over the water bowl. 'But it can wait.'

'No, it can't,' Claudia said impatiently. 'You and I have learned not to put things off. We can never be sure what's around the corner, right?' The dog barked and Claudia laughed. 'Look who agrees. You tell him, boy.' Midnight barked again and chased his tail in a dizzying circle, forcing Claudia's familiar cackle to erupt.

I can't tell her now, Ben thought as he saw the dark-haired beauty with the big smile he'd fallen for the night of the dance. He couldn't ignore his plan. He'd be risking losing a friendship more vital to him than air.

'Midnight and I should go,' he said, attempting to drag the collarless dog up the hallway. 'Someone's got a date with the bathtub and clippers tomorrow. Don't you, buddy?'

At that, Midnight startled them both, breaking away and charging Ben's forgotten backpack on the floor by the fireplace.

'Oh, look, Ben, he's reminding you to take your bag. Clever boy, Midnight.'

'Yeah, real cute. Get your snout out of there, you nosey mutt.'

But Midnight buried his head further inside the bag and in the melee between man and beast, Ben lost; his six-foot frame taken down by the polished floorboards, his shoulder smarting from the awkward landing.

'What's this Ben Ledson?' Claudia stood motionless, the box she'd snatched from Midnight's mouth in her hand, her face morphing from wide-eyed surprise to a suspicious squint. 'Is this to do with your big news? Is this for some girl? Do I know her?'

'Umm.' Ben dragged his body back to standing as Claudia opened the small box. 'Yes, no, maybe, or not exactly. I, ah—'

She laughed. 'No surprise you're still single, Ben. Make up your mind. Is it or isn't it for some lucky girl?'

She looped the twisted gold chain over her index finger, raising the oval-shaped locket to the light so the gold glimmered like Claudia had shone at the dance.

'Depends,' Ben replied. He'd been carrying the box for weeks, waiting for the right time. 'Do you like it, Claud?'

'Of course! You have excellent taste. In fact, it's so divine, if you don't tell me who the lucky girl is I'll keep it for myself. Midnight brought the box right to me.'

'Because it's yours—if you want,' Ben said.

Her cocky grin faded. 'Oh, no, I … I was joking.'

'But I'm not.' Ben rubbed a hand across the back of his neck to massage away the tension. Whatever the time, whatever the stage in his project, it was now or never. 'It's a locket watch,' he announced. 'There's an inscription inside.'

Claudia peeled the lid back. '*For when the time's right.*' Looking from the inscription to Ben, she asked, 'What does that mean?'

He squared his shoulders to steady himself and after a deep breath to clear his head explained. 'I bought it a while back. I've been carting the box around, waiting for the right time to tell you.'

'Tell me what?'

She wasn't making this easy, standing there in her pink pyjama pants and singlet top, her big blue eyes blinking in time with Ben's heartbeat. No one had ever taken his breath away like Claudia and the synchronicity between them had always staggered him. He dropped his gaze, concentrating instead on the tip of his thong stubbing a polished knot in the floorboards.

He gulped hard—twice—and muttered, 'I treasure our friendship, Claud, and I'm aware you loved Jack. I miss him too. Hell, we grew up together, more brothers really, and yet, there was so much about him I never knew. So much he never knew.' Claudia was staring, her head cocked, curious. 'But I know one thing. A guy doesn't make a move on a mate's girl, even though I had dibs on you first. And let me tell you, Claud, I was bloody pissed off with Jack that night— and he knew it. But you liked him. All the girls did. To them, Jack was the bachelor to catch and, well ...' A small snort and a smile interrupted his monologue. 'He was crazy about you on the night so I—'

'Whoa, back up, Ben Ledson!' Claudia looked mad. 'What do you mean you had dibs on me?'

'Ah, wow, look at the time.' This was exactly what Ben had feared. 'I shouldn't do this now. It's late and I've upset you. I need to go.'

'Oh, so, all of a sudden you're worried about the late hour?' Claudia wrapped her arms across her chest. 'You're staying put, Ben Ledson, until you've told me what's going on. Sit.' Both Ben and Midnight obeyed the command, sitting in unison—Ben on a dining chair and Midnight by his feet. 'Now,' she said, her eyes fixed on Ben's. 'Speak.'

'Well, I, ah … On the night of the ball, me and Jack and you and … What was her name?'

'Lucy. Stop stalling.'

'Okay, so it's not what men should do—and I don't any longer,' he clarified. 'But since we were kids, Jack ruled and the rest of us blokes followed. I was stoked when he picked Lucy straight up that night. My mistake was telling him because, Jack being Jack …' Ben shrugged. 'He goes and changes his mind. That's when I went home.'

'You left me and Lucy with Jack? Why, Ben? Why not stand up to him?'

'Because I learned a long time ago, when you hang with guys like Jack, the score is always the same. Superhero: two. Nerdy sidekick: zero. At least, that's what I once thought.'

Claudia nodded. 'Somehow, Jack got away with being a dickhead. Even I let him,' she spoke to the pendant in her hands, then at Ben, a small smile dragging her lips into a sheepish curl at the corners. 'If only you'd stayed. I wasn't at all into Jack that night. I wasn't sure he was really into me. Jack always had a way about him that made me wonder if … Anyway, I wasn't as keen on him as he seemed to be on me. I may have even told Lucy I had dibs on you. When you took off I figured you weren't interested, and with Lucy not keen on Jack, well …' She looked straight at him. 'I guess I …'

The pair was silent for several loud ticks of the grandfather clock.

'Good grief, Ben! Why haven't you said anything before now?'

'I was waiting until you were ready for someone else.'

'Oh Ben,' she said, tossing her head back and delivering her best Claudia cackle. 'I was waiting for you to hit on me. Imagine if Midnight hadn't come home and dug this out of your bag. I might still be waiting.' She knelt and cuddled the dog in a bear hug. 'I think I might like dogs again.'

'Are you serious, Claud?'

'Of course. Your knock on the door woke me at 11:11 pm on the dot. That must be a sign. The universe is reminding us both to pay attention to our hearts, to our souls, and to our inner selves.'

'You mean my timing doesn't suck?'

'No, Ben, in fact ...' Claudia again popped the locket cover open. 'It's way past time. Can we agree to stop wasting anymore and make tomorrow about us?'

'And about Midnight?' Ben asked.

'Yes, and about Midnight.'

LOST IN LINGERIE

The morning drags on. The clock on the wall clicks over to 11:11 am and I'm already thinking about food. Twice I've checked my ruby red lipstick, fluffed the blonde wisps of my pixie cut into place over my ears, and untangled the dangling bits of my earrings. I'm contemplating a quick trip to the loo when I see him.

He's in ladies' lingerie—the fourth man I've seen this week. Monday's bloke had been young and obviously unsettled by the flurry of frilly knickers. Tuesday had delivered a grey-haired husband who'd appeared tired and disinterested—no doubt after decades of the same change room waiting game. Obedient and obliging, he'd whistled a repertoire of tunes while his wife fitted her double-Ds into a C cup while calling for more garments in different colours. Wednesday's stately gent, overwhelmed by choice, had stayed less than a minute before walking out in a huff. But no man in my ten years at W. C. Chedwick & Co. had looked more lost in lingerie than today's black-haired hunk with the Akubra hat and a big-buckled belt, adrift between the maternity bras and control briefs and with a bemused expression.

I pinch back my grin and approach with caution. 'Hello! May I assist?'

'I, ah, need a bra,' he says. 'Today.'

'You've come to the right department!' With my professional mask in place, I can't help wondering if this customer will be the one to break my record of the most weirdos in a single week? 'Something in particular?' I enquire.

'Pink.' He coughs the word into his hand. 'Pretty, you know?'

'Yes, sure, pink! Let me check.' I scan the rack and notice an abundance of black, beige and blue. White is rife, but no pink. 'I'm afraid we have none in stock. Pink is very in with the ladies at the moment and it's been busy, what with the rush to grab a bargain for Valentine's Day on the weekend I—'

'Oh, no,' he says, 'this isn't for a lady and there is no Valentine's Day rush.'

'Okey dokey! That makes things easier.' I try to sound positive. 'I can order what you need from the catalogue. A Friday order will mean delivery in ten days.'

'Ten?' His expression is one of panic as he runs a hand through the thick mop of black hair. 'No, ordering something definitely won't do.'

'Another colour perhaps? A lady always appreciates something white and lacy. You can't go wrong with—'

'It's not so simple. I told you, this isn't for a lady and I can't be waiting ten days.' Desperation darkens his face. 'I need a pink bra —today.'

'A bra! Pink! Today? Okay!' I espy the CCTV camera covering the store and, for the first time, wish there was a real person sitting behind a monitor, poised to act should the pink-bra-weirdo guy turn aggressive. 'Let me see. Ah, yes.'

I'm soon elbow-deep in the discount bin overflowing with stock and lost among the ridiculously small, the outrageous, the gaudy, the wicked, and the bewildering underwear designs left over from last season. Then I spot a single satin bra, the colour of fairy floss. At the garment's centre, and on both straps, sits a decorative daisy-shaped button.

'It's only 12 double A.' My jargon is inconsiderate. His quizzical brow says as much. 'What I mean is, a 12 double A is tiny. Both the cup and the—'

'Looks fine,' he mutters, his hand ferreting a wallet from his back pocket. 'Can I take it with me now?'

'Sure!' I nod while hiding my amusement. Of course he can take it with him. *We're not talking about a new car!* 'Follow me to the service desk, sir.'

After I've dropped the bra into a bag, the customer relaxes. Then he fumbles the credit card, and it whizzes across the paper bags on the counter.

'Sorry, this is my first time and—'

'Oh, please,' I say, maintaining good eye contact. 'There is no need to explain. My job is to help every customer.' I'm not sure why, but I check the card for a signature. The writing is neat and guarded, like him, I suspect. 'Thank you, Mr Davis. I hope your purchase does the trick.'

'Me too.' He forces an uncertain smile to match the uncertainty in his voice and pauses as if he might say something else. In the end, the expression in his eyes, and not his words, conveys appreciation.

Once he's gone, my routine returns and I smile, my mood lifted; perhaps because I'll have a story to tell my best friend tonight. As usual, I'll find Ginny waiting for me near the pub on the corner, insisting I need a drink, a night out—a life.

U

Tanglewood Pub draws all sorts on a Friday evening. Among the lonesome, the lovers, and those seeking a no-strings lay is the worker hoping to wind down, like me, and farmers who need to chat about their week. Tonight, it seems everyone in town has come to hear the band or to enjoy the weekly *Steak 'n' Schnitty* meal deal. Regulars prop up their spot at the bar, while others gather around tables or lounge in booths.

I'm perched on one of three stools by the fire, with Ginny by my side. For reasons unknown, my friend has chosen a different vantage point tonight, and since arriving she's had one eye on the door, her excitement obvious in the speed with which she chatters. Whenever we get together, Ginny does most of the talking. Not that I mind. Running the local post office, being privy to the town's gossip and goings-on, makes her a far better storyteller than I could ever be. Whatever the reason tonight, her enthusiasm is a contagion I welcome after a long week. Laughing with Ginny feels as good as the cool river of crimson-coloured wine coursing down my throat.

When my friend pauses to nibble the handful of bar snacks, I fill in the void by mentioning pink-bra-weirdo guy. I'm only part way through my story when Ginny's obvious disinterest stops me.

'What's got into you tonight?' I ask, following her gaze.

Ginny gasps from behind her hand. 'He came! Oh my gosh, don't look, Tina, he'll see you. How's my hair?'

'Beautiful,' I assure her. 'As usual.'

While my best friend preps and preens in anticipation, I consider checking my own appearance, sucking in my stomach and wishing I'd shaved my legs and reapplied my lipstick.

'Who is this guy I'm not supposed to notice, Gin-gin?' I ask.

'The one I mentioned last week, or course. The stockyard's new supervisor.' Ginny's checks her bared teeth with the tip of her little finger, flicks her Farrah-Fawcett-is-back-in-fashion hair, and crosses slender, silken legs while tugging on the hem of her tube-like miniskirt. 'I so hoped he'd come. I've been dying for you to meet. His name means warrior and … Oh my gosh, he's so cute. You can look now. He's with the security guy by the door.'

Surprise sucks the smile from my face. The guys eyes are what I notice first. They're loaded with the same uncertainty and sadness I'd witnessed this afternoon.

'I can't believe it's him, Ginny.'

'Hmm?' My friend feigns interest 'Did you say something, sweetie?' Ginny sees only her warrior as she smacks perfectly painted lips together, adjusts the cleavage in her tank top and sings out across the crowded bar area. 'Who-hoo! Over here.'

'But, Ginny … Ginny it's him,' I tell her hurriedly. 'The guy from the Ladies' Lingerie section this morning.'

I finally have all her attention. 'My Kian, the guy covered in tattoos, is your daisy-bra-weirdo guy?'

'Kian?' I query.

'So hot, don't you reckon?' she says, while sexy-swivelling on her stool. 'Did I mention the name's Irish? Wait until you hear his accent.'

'Accent? No, no. Not the tattoos.' The two men are en route so I talk without moving my lips, my jaw clenched. 'The one *with* Kian.' The sad-eyed man, I want to tell her. The one looking self-conscious. The one walking this way.

'Hey there, me beautiful girl,' Kian croons. 'This here's me buddy, Mick Davis. I told ya 'bout him, remember, Gin? And you must be Tina. Am I right?' Irish eyes smile at me.

Ginny answers for me with a nudge. 'Sure is. She's my very lovely and extremely single friend, Tina. Say hello to the boys.'

'Err, hello, boys!'

Is there a trace of recognition in Mick's double take, and is it delight or discomfiture? Or, like me, is it a desperate desire to avoid what is most definitely a set-up? Mick and I exchange polite smiles and he seems regular enough in the familiar surroundings of a pub and without the fashionable forest of frilly underwear. Gone is the earlier man-on-the-land look. Mick's hat hair is spiked with styling gel, his face clean-shaven and shiny, and his body looks taut under a T-shirt and blue jeans.

On a corner stage, a country crooner is tuning his guitar strings, adding to the cacophonous pub crowd. When the jarring noise of speaker feedback splits the air, all four of us head to an empty U-shaped booth at the far end of the room. Ginny attaches herself to Kian's arm and hangs on his every word, while I trail behind with daisy-bra-weirdo guy silent at my side. I assume, as there's no mention of our encounter at the store, I am not so memorable and stick instead to pleasantries, platitudes, and other perfunctory pub chat. He's nice, I decide. He's different and intense, but best of all, he's not weird. Now, if I can only stop picturing Mick in the pink bra with the little daisies.

U

Two hours of talk and two bourbons later, Mick is laughing at one of my jokes when I realise what had been missing from his face at the store today. It's the same thing missing from my life.

Joy.

The band takes a break and a woman, sweaty from dancing, squeezes on the end of the booth. As Mick and I shift along to make room, our arms and shoulders touch and I sense warmth, smell cologne, and hear … *Justin Bieber?*

He reaches into a pocket to claim the ringtone and listens to the caller before his expression shifts to something inscrutable: too sad to be a smile and not sad enough to say tragedy. Confusion perhaps?

'Sorry, gotta go,' he says in a rush.

And he does. No explanation. Nothing. Gone.

I shrug at Ginny and offer her my famous will-you-finally-admit-I'm-a-hopeless-case-and-give-up-on-me look, while disappointment grinds my voice flat. 'Was it something I said?'

'Excuse my friend, ladies,' Kian butts in. 'Mick's new in town and he's got a few, ah, issues to work through.'

More than you know, I want to tell him. I don't.

I move from the seat, deciding to call it a night until Ginny's expression says please, don't. So, like the good and loyal friend I am, I settle in and sip more water.

'Poor bloke's shattered,' Kian continues. 'Life can be a pile o'shite, to be sure, and poor ol' Mick's had a heap piled on him in the worst possible way.'

'What's wrong?' Ginny asks.

'Lost his wife twelve months ago in a car crash in the city. Only him and Evie these days. They moved bush hoping for a fresh start and time to heal after the mine offered him an onsite management role. Good bloke, ol' Mick.'

Kian's voice is soft, and I glimpse the man behind the pretentiousness. He's sensitive and so syrupy I can almost hear Ginny falling further in love with him.

Lucky her!

'Only one way forward if you were to ask me. That's to get right back in the saddle, if you know what I mean.' Macho Kian is back. 'I've been threatening to drag him to the pub for ages. Tonight, out of the blue, he agrees.'

My curiosity piques. 'Who's Evie?'

'His daughter. She's thirteen. Imagine! I'd be effin' mortified if I had a teenager ask me the stuff she asks her dad.'

I'm instantly intrigued. 'Stuff? Like what?'

'Girl stuff. Losing a mum's tough on the kid, but, man-o-man, there are things a bloke should never have to cop—or buy.' Kian grimaces and fakes a shudder. 'The school sports carnival is on next week and Mick tells me most other girls in the locker room with Evie are … Well, they have you-know-whats?' He cups pretend breasts at his chest.

'Boobs!' Ginny's interpretation is unnecessary, but very Ginny.

'Yeah, boobs, and bras to go with 'em,' Kian continues. 'Now, ladies, forgive me, but I always thought a bra was a bra—and better off than on.' He winks and Ginny turns scarlet. 'But Evie's been so desperate to make school friends, she's gone and got herself involved with a group of girls whose Secret Social Club colour is pink. Everything—and I mean everything—has to be pink. "The pinker the better", poor Mick told me last week.'

'Pink?' Ginny hoots. 'Tina and I were all grunge and camouflage pants. Remember, Teens? Bras optional.'

'Now you're talking my language, beautiful. But these friends of Evie's call 'emselves Pinkalicious, which leaves poor Mick promising to find his daughter a—'

'Pink bra?' My announcement silences the duo until Kian's mobile beeps.

'Speak o' the devil. It's a message from Mick.' A few finger taps and he's grinning. 'And it's for you, Tina.'

'Me?' I turn towards Ginny whose face has that aren't-I-clever-setting-you-up-with-this-one smile.

'Reckon the bloke might have finally lost his marbles though. Do you understand the message?' Kian passes me the phone, only to have Ginny intercept the device midair.

'Let me see.' First, she frowns. Then her eyebrows arch.

'What?' I ask anxiously. 'Out with it, Ginny.'

'He says, "Tell Tina thx. Sorry to run. Can I …?" Ginny's eyes bug open.

'What?' I'm pleading, my heart banging inside my chest. 'Can he what?'

'It reads: "Can I meet you in ladies' underwear sometime?"'

Kian roars with laughter and recovers his phone from my bemused best friend. 'Want me to reply for you, Tina?'

'Yes.' I settle smugly in my seat. 'Just tell him—yes.'

A SUITCASE BY THE DOOR

Although I remember little about that night, one memory refusing to fade is the enormousness of those hands as they wound the thin rope too tight and tugged too hard on my tiny frame. Shoved onto the backseat of a strange-smelling car, my first instinct was to curl my body into the smallest shape possible and wait without making a sound.

I should have felt utterly terrified—I would nowadays—but back then I'd been too young to grasp how cruel people could be. I recall questioning why anyone would take me away from my family, only to abandon me on a muggy midsummer's night and lock me inside a dank old shack. How long I remained there, overwhelmed by the fetid odour of decay—escape impossible—I don't know. All I recall is a high dust-smeared windowpane masking the moonlight; the tree limbs enlivened by wind gusts smacking against the building; and the smell of eucalypt—of the Australian bush—telling me I was a long way from home.

When fear did finally wriggle its way into my thoughts, I closed my eyes to stop the shadowy silhouettes that crept over walls from morphing into monsters. But there was no blocking the deafening torrent on the tin roof. That's when I knew one thing. I would always hate the rain.

I can't be sure how long I waited for someone to hear my pleas for help. I only know my nightmare ended the day Damien came into my life; so did the rain.

With the sun shining bright and warm through the open door, he'd walked over, crouched beside me in his skin-tight shorts and T-shirt, and calmly told me, 'You're okay now. Come on, let's get you out of here.'

I recall staring in disbelief—first at his kind face, then at his helmet with its spikey crown of long black cable ties.

'Stops the magpies swooping,' he explained through a smile. 'They don't like me and my bike very much.'

◡

Five years later, I cannot understand the magpie's dislike of a person as terrific as Damien; the man who taught me to trust again and brought colour to a world that once held nothing more than grim shades of grey. Days with Damien are a lot like rainbows—always the same and yet always a surprise, but with one exception … Tonight.

Tonight, the man in my life—my rescuer and best friend—came home from work, kicked off his shoes, and changed out of his suit. After eating together in the small kitchen of our Alexandria townhouse, we settled in the living room for some mind-numbing television, my head in Damien's lap while he snoozed. Of course he did. After five years, there is nothing I don't know about this man. There isn't an expression on his face, a tone in his voice, or a shade in his mood I don't understand. Except for tonight. After dinner, Damien usually snoozed in the stately old chair—the best seat in the house— his hand resting heavily across my shoulders. But something about his silence unsettles me. The television is on, creating a vivid lightshow on the walls, but I prefer watching Damien, waiting for a shift in the rise and fall of his chest to signal he's waking. When he does, I lift my gaze to his and see an arching bushy brow drag one sleepy eyelid open. He smiles, knowing he's done it again, and squints at his watch in the semi-dark.

'It's 11:11 pm, Jess. You should've woken me. Come on, best get to bed before we both turn into pumpkins.'

There's never an argument from me. My absolute favourite time with Damien is snuggling in bed at night when the lights go off and nothing else matters. It's during those final awake moments in the dark together—knowing I'm safe and loved—that wrongs are forgotten, any misdemeanours forgiven. His caress is so comforting I can fall asleep, finally unafraid of shadows.

It's barely light when Damien leaves the bed, his socked feet padding over the floorboards. The click of a latch and the creaking door tells me I should get up, take an interest, see what he's doing in the spare room, but the cool morning air quickly quashes the thought and I stretch before curling my body into a tight ball.

Just a little longer.

Startled from my half-sleep when Damien sits on the edge of the mattress, I lift my head and squint at him through one eye.

'Hey there, gorgeous!' He slaps me routinely on my butt and taps a finger to my nose. 'Time to get a move on, sleepyhead.'

I don't make a peep, preferring to let my eyes speak, pleading for a few more minutes. Waking up has never come easily, and I'm definitely no good for anything before breakfast.

'Come on, Jess.' He stands, shifts to the foot of the bed, arms crossed in a don't-mess-with-me manner. 'We talked about this, remember? Let's go and get it over with.'

Did I remember? Are we going somewhere?

The day outside the bedroom window is dull, the sky a gloomy grey like my mood. My disposition only worsens when I pad down the hall to find a suitcase by the door. The bag had been a gift; a big hint from his mother to ditch a girlfriend and come home to the country. But Damien didn't dump her. He didn't have to. Within a month, the girlfriend had left him.

Zippers! That's it! The sound I'd heard in my half-sleep earlier had been the zip of a suitcase closing. I shivered. If there's anything I remember from my life before Damien it was the rasping sound of packing tape and a relentless racket of zippers—the tiny sounds that scream someone is going somewhere or leaving someone.

I lift my head to glance outside. The gloomy sky has turned gunmetal grey and the dusty scent of early rain twitches my nose. I've never trusted rainy days and now dread what lies ahead. I don't want to say goodbye to Damien. I can't lose him. He's my life, my best friend. He's my rainbow after a storm: consistent, reliable, beautiful. I need that. I need my wonderful and routine existence. I need Damien and I thought Damien needed me. I want to scream at him: *I've loved you, and only you all these years and without expectation, and this is how you love me back?* But I don't make a sound. The jarring noise I hear is the suitcase shrieking its warning.

I could protest, but I rarely do, preferring to trust he'll understand my trepidation and change his mind, as usual. If only Damien's reactions didn't confuse me at times. I've seen him in a rage over the smallest thing, like when I inadvertently knocked his glass off the coffee table and red wine stained the rug.

Now, there's a packed suitcase at the front door and he's waiting for me. How do I tell him I don't want to leave? I've got a bad feeling about driving anywhere with him this morning and there's a moment I consider challenging Damien. A moment until my courage wanes and I walk to the car and climb into the passenger seat.

Relaxing is not easy as Damien speeds through the deserted early morning streets, a little crazed and unusually anxious. Soothing him after a stressful day at work is second nature to me, but something is off. If only he'd talk, tell me what's going on. We've never had trouble communicating in the past. But with no idea where we are, or where we're going, confusion soon dominates my every emotion.

Soon the roads narrow, suburbia's bricks and mortar and manicured lawns replaced by unruly trees, their thick trunks rising out of roadside weed beds. As we speed past the long grasses lurching and waving us on, my stomach also lurches, my wooziness worsening with each bend. Damien must sense something because the passenger window slides open. I want to acknowledge the gesture and reach out in the hope my touch will slow him down, but he won't look at me.

'Not now, Jess, please.' He brushes me away, turns the volume up on the radio, drives faster.

The music is loud. So loud my ears hurt, but I find solace in the cool, scented wind rushing past my face as I lean into the open window, my eyes closed, my mind imagining I'm somewhere else, somewhere safe, somewhere with rainbows.

The car slows, and Damien steers a sharp left onto a gravel road, as the tyres whip up plumes of dust. *Is this it? Is this where my happy life with Damien ends?* We're tearing through unfamiliar terrain, passing small tumbledown shacks and a maze of high fences, and my nails grip so tight they dent the doorsill's soft leather. After turning off the highway, the car rattles along a narrow track and stops outside a tumbledown shed.

When a bulky man approaches, holding a coiled rope and hessian sack in strong, work-weary hands, I glance at Damien. I want him to see the fear in my eyes. I want to remind him: *You saved me once. You found me, took me home, loved me and let me love you back. You promised you'd never abandon me. You can turn the car around and save me again, Damien. Please turn the car around.*

'You knew this day might come, Jess. Please don't hate me.'

His palm caresses the side of my face and I lean my head into it, desperate to show him I'm not capable of hate, and urging him to read my mind and understand my fear, he pulls away and slams both fists against the steering wheel.

'Don't look at me, Jess, you know I'm a sucker for your eyes.' His stare is fierce as he presses an arm against my chest, pushing me back into the seat. 'Just stay here.' He scrambles out of the driver's door and rushes to the other side of the car, yelling, but it's too late. The man with the rope has my door open, his big hands grabbing the beautiful hair Damien loves to brush. I want to cry out but manage only a pitiful whimper.

'Mate, hang on.' Damien grabs the man's hand. 'I've changed my mind. I'm not leaving her here with you. I might've paid a premium for your *premium* services and I thought I could go through with this, but I can't. Keep the money, okay. I'm taking her with me. I'll find another way.'

The man seems amused, his laugh mocking. 'Good luck doin' that on a long weekend.'

A few minutes later Damien is behind the wheel and speeding back towards the highway.

'Jessie, you're making me late. Why did you look at me when I told you not to? Why do you always make it so hard for me to leave you?' He reaches across, his face tinged with regret as he brushes the hair from my eyes. Although his touch comforts me, I tremble. 'Not talking to me, eh? I'm not surprised.' His finger taps the tip of my nose, and I do my best to show him a smile. 'I'll make it up to you, Jess, I promise.'

We drive in silence, the mobile telephone occupying Damien for most of the journey.

When we finally stop, it's outside a small cottage nestled between trees. A woman is waving from the doorway, a smart-looking red setter obedient by her side.

'You made it, Damo! I was worrying you wouldn't.'

'I have a tale to tell,' Damien replies as he again leaves me behind in the car.

I'm confused and worried and itch to be set free. The smell of mown grass is so intoxicating I can't wait to get out of the car and pee. But Damien is holding up a flat palm and mouthing the word, *Stay*.

I obey. I always do even though my skin bristles as he gives the red-haired dog a rough-and-tumble pat while kissing the pretty woman.

'Your text message was well timed,' she tells him. 'I was about to drop Red at my sister's but this is a much better idea.'

'You don't mind spending our romantic weekend with the dogs?' he asks. 'A kennel with a hessian sack for a bed is no place for my Jessie-girl.'

'Marcia told me you're a soft touch, Damo. We like that in a man, don't we Red?' She ruffles her dog's ears. 'I've never heard of Tanglewood. How did you find this Wagtail Cottage place? A guesthouse this nice and welcoming dogs in rooms is rare.'

'Google,' Damien replies. 'Not sure why I didn't think to do it before, or why I forgot my furry mate is part of who I am. I'm a textbook case of love me, love my dog.'

They kiss again and I'm relieved to see the old Damien, the happy Damien, the de-stressed Damien of old I know and love.

'C'mon Jess,' Damien finally whistles and walks towards to the car. 'Time to say hello.'

As I prepare to launch myself from the passenger seat, I look skyward. There are no longer grey skies or signs of rain. Only a rainbow.

One Friday in
Sunflower

Swept Away

A Penny for your Thoughts

Geronimo

The Male Run

Some Days are Diamonds

'Reading is my favorite occupation, when I have leisure for it
and books to read.'

— ANNE BRONTË

SWEPT AWAY

It's life's special moments that usually flashed before a person's eyes moments before death. Sally O'Neill saw only headlines:
Intrepid Reporter Swept to Her Death
Media Maverick Dies—Microphone in Hand
Washed Up Before She's Even Begun

Sally knew she was in trouble the second the runaway rubber dinghy slammed into the back of her knees, buckling them. Then, much like a teaspoon might rescue a drowning bug, the out-of-control craft scooped Sally up, tossing her so she landed on her back, legs and arms flailing. Quick to steady herself on all fours, her ears straining to hear Liam's words over the rush of floodwaters, she watched as specks of orange-clad emergency services personnel scattered.

'Just hold on,' her trusty cameraman called. 'We. Will. Find. You.'

U

As the boat bumped to a stop, and Sally's head slammed into the hard rubber bow, brown water surged, sloshing over the gunwales to

55

muddy her beige jeans and the red businesslike shirt she favoured for on-camera work. There was, however, far more to worry about than her soggy state of dress. 'I'm sinking!'

'No, you're not.'

Startled, Sally sat upright and squinted at the figure towering overhead, his bulk a silhouette against a glary sky.

'Sally O'Neill, I presume?' the man asked. 'Heard you might pass by.'

'Pass by?' Sally prickled at the casual comment and attempted to stand until a dizzy spell and a head pain stopped her.

'You've bumped your head badly,' the man said. 'Let me ...'

Before she could object, he'd plucked her from the boat, and was carrying her up a forested hillside with its leafy canopy offering intermittent relief from the stabbing shards of sunlight.

'I'll be fine. Really,' Sally said as the wooden cabin with a bullnose veranda came into view. But was she assuring him or herself? 'I *can* walk,' she insisted. *I can run, too*, she added silently.

'Almost there,' he said. 'You can sit for a bit and I'll find a bandaid for your forehead.'

Sally instinctively touched her forehead while examining the man's face, but the broad brim of the stranger's Akubra hat hid all but the perspiration sprinkles on a five o'clock shadow and a butt-chin that put John Travolta's dimple to shame.

'Where's Liam?' she asked. 'Where's my cameraman?'

'Probably preparing to wait this inundation out with locals at the Sunflower pub.'

On the veranda with its creaking boards, the man gently lowered Sally until she was sitting on a wooden plank supported by two plastic crates butted up against the building's blistered paintwork.

Conscious of wet fabric clinging to her every curve, Sally plucked at the sodden cotton shirt. 'And where am I?'

'A few hundred metres short of Deadman's Hollow.'

'Deadman's Hollow?' Barely able to blink her water-laden lashes, Sally tried convincing herself she hadn't drifted into a watery Wolf Creek sequel, but as fear snaked its way through her body, her arms deadened with cold and her jaw shuddered. *Don't be ridiculous*, she told herself. This man has just saved you. Deranged killers don't live on the outskirts of towns named Sunflower, and they sure as heck don't rescue people. Do they?

'Wait here,' he told her. 'I'll grab towels.'

'T-t-t-towels, yes, g-g-g-good, you do-do that.'

As both a journalist and a keen observer of other people's lives, Sally took the opportunity to forensically investigate her surroundings: the dark corners of a cobweb-covered bullnose awning, massive mauve flowers hanging from a tangle of vines strangling six support posts and, against the wall of the house, a weather-beaten table holding wax-dripped wine bottles, miscellaneous matchboxes, and a stack of tatty magazines. Balanced along the handrail was a garden of sorts, with miscellaneous pots, old boots, small buckets, and margarine tubs containing rock and succulent displays, while on the veranda boards below, something herbaceous sprouted from egg cartons and cardboard toilet rolls filled with soil.

Trust me to find the only plant-propagating psychopath on the planet. This guy wastes nothing!

'Reuse and recycle,' the man said, as if hearing her thoughts. 'Single use is for the selfish and the squanderers of the world.'

A recycling sociopath, Sally silently corrected. One with almost iridescent green eyes. With him having discarded his Akubra, his face was visible and she could see his brown hair was slicked back and knotted into a man bun.

'Feeling any better?' he asked.

'Yes, much.' Sally sipped twice from the glass he handed her before cradling the drink on her lap. The liquid rippled from an incontrollable quiver as she mentally replayed what had surely been a near-death experience. Who knows where she might've ended up if the dinghy had kept going. *Deadman's Hollow?* Overwhelmed by the thought, Sally suddenly squeaked out three words. 'You. Saved. Me.' They sounded pathetic somehow. They were utterly true.

The man smiled, almost laughed. 'And you saved *me* a lengthy walk to Deadman's—or a swim—and I had no time, nor the inclination, to dress for either scenario.' He stepped back and Sally noticed he'd changed into a dry T-shirt and a pair of patterned board shorts. 'To describe what I did as anything more dramatic would sound like a reporter sensationalising an otherwise unremarkable rescue. But come to think of it,' he added, 'I'm not sure I've had the privilege of saving a damsel in distress before today'.

He didn't seem to notice Sally snap to attention as she readied to defend her profession. 'Two things,' she began. 'One, not every journalist sensationalises their stories; two, I can assure you I have never been, nor will I ever be a damsel—either in distress, or otherwise.'

A trace of amusement loosened the man's lips into a broader smile. 'Well, had your boat ventured down the main river and not the smaller south arm which normally trickles by my back paddock, the outcome might've been different. Luckily for you, the SES Commander phoned to advise that one of their boats broke free and collected a news reporter. He told me to keep an eye out and advise him if you showed up.'

'If? That's a bit casual, isn't it?' Snatching a fresh towel from the pile on an adjacent seat, Sally patted her arms and dabbed her face. *If I showed up?* She grumbled to herself while strangling an impromptu ponytail of sodden hair, then twisting the bulk of black curls into a messy knot at her nape. 'People are coming to get me, right?'

'Eventually,' he said while twisting an old cane rocking chair around and sitting to face her. 'The crew has bigger issues upstream. A section of bank gave way, uprooting trees and sending a surge of river water and debris down river. The debris was responsible for sling-shotting the rubber dinghy from one side to the other and into you. It's a real mess. I contacted them just now; advised you were safe and not to hurry.'

Frustration forced Sally to her feet. 'Not hurry? I can't wait around like this. There's research, a story to produce, and … And look at me!'

Mud coated her clothes and her hair had dripped slime over the shirt, thanks to the new styling gel that supposedly guaranteed all-day definition and shine for corkscrew curls. *Ha!* Even the sharp puff of breath from the corner of her mouth failed to shift the irksome, waterlogged helix of black dangling over one eye. All this because, against her better judgement, she'd waded into a flooded causeway to put the emergency services people rescuing a bogged cow into the camera's frame, hoping an interesting backdrop would impress the boss. Despite the shin-deep water, the causeway had seemed safe, the current reasonably slow until a cracking sound upstream had caused a flurry of activity with the SES crew and their stuck cow. Keen to capture the action, Sally had signalled Liam to start filming. If only she'd stuck to the original assignment, rather than trying to combine the greedy corporate Goliath story with a report about climate change and severe storms up north causing flash flooding in numerous riverside towns. The Sunflower Community Action Group was speaking out about controversial mining proposals, with one resident claiming on Facebook the mine operation had negatively affected water catchments and forced the normally lazy river to split into several determined and fast-flowing tributaries.

And that was how a dinghy had swept Sally away and stranded her with the stranger who seemed amused by her wringing water from her sneakers and socks.

'You're staring,' she blurted.

'You said "look at me". I am. Looking.'

While conceding some women might find his chin cleft and smile disarming, Sally was in no mood to be charmed, nor to be charming.

'I was referring to my work clothes,' she clarified, plonking herself back down onto the plank seat. 'This is—was—my best shirt.'

'I wouldn't have thought our little inundation warranted an on-the-spot TV crew.'

'You call this a little inundation?' Sally's gaze swept over the inland sea surrounding the knoll—partly green, mostly junkyard—currently keeping them and the cabin high and dry, at least for the time being.

The man shrugged. 'It's deluge or drought out here.' He stepped closer. 'Farming is hard work made harder still by Mother Nature. And our politicians reckon there's no such thing as climate change. Idiots! Just as well country folk are resilient and get on with the job.'

'Not without a lot of heartache and stress,' Sally said. 'Stock losses must be devastating at any time, but when animals are your livelihood … I can't imagine.'

'Like I said, we unite when times are tough, and towns like Sunflower bounce back because we have other, less weather-dependent industry bolstering the local economy.'

'United is not the word I'm hearing in the lead-up to tomorrow's shareholder's rally at the mine. The AGM is the actual reason I've come to town.'

'I've heard there will be a number of reporters, journalists, and the usual agitators. Surely you have more interesting stories to cover.'

Yes, more interesting, she might have replied, but this story was the lucky break Sally needed. 'Two powerful and opposing arguments regarding mining operations makes Ruby Garnet Mines newsworthy indeed,' she told him. 'Both camps expect to hear from the CEO, although my research suggests he won't show.'

'You have a researcher?' he asked.

'No, that's not what I meant. I prefer to do my own, and yeah, I've sussed out the CEO. He keeps a fairly low profile. Leaves all the upfront stuff to his people.'

'His people?' he queried.

'Yeah, you know.' Sally's curled fingers jabbed at the air to help make her point. 'I'll have my "people" phone your "people". *Gah!* Snootiness on any scale riles me. I can't stand the way pretentious people delight in making the rest of us feel mediocre.'

'Do they?' he asked. 'Do you feel mediocre?'

Sally shrugged, mainly because she had no answer and her headache hurt too much to make her think of one. She was also embarrassed. Why *did* wealthy, successful types make her feel anything, especially inferior? More to the point, why the need to confess to a stranger who minutes earlier she'd considered a psychopath?

'It's the CEO's minders who annoy me,' she clarified. 'I hear they're picky about who gets the one-on-one interviews.'

'I suppose that's the job of a minder,' he quipped. 'They choose the best person.'

And therein lies the problem, she might have told him. No one chooses her for anything. She wasn't even the first choice for this assignment in Sunflower.

'Well, I wouldn't mind getting a scoop. Small would do. Something to impress the boss. But the guy does few on-camera interviews. Mostly magazine stuff: *BRW* and business publications. An article last year showed him silhouetted against the window of his Sydney skyscraper. The entire top three floors are one lavish apartment.'

'Lavish!' he responded, his pitch a notch higher. 'All three? Sounds excessive.'

'Tell me about it!' Sally replied. 'And tell me this. Why do we need such detail or his remarkable wealth shoved in our very unremarkable faces? Why do the rich intrigue the ordinary people? I know the answer, of course,' she added.

'Well, now you have *me* intrigued. Care to share?'

Sally did the extraordinary. With his smile warming, the tiny tilt of his head endearing, and the lilt in his voice encouraging, she felt safe to share her thoughts on the matter of the rich and arrogant. It's not like she would bump into him again.

'To most of us,' she began, 'an extravagant lifestyle is out of reach. But we are human beings and people are programmed to want what they can't have. The grass is greener, and all that jazz,' she said with a flurry of jazz hands. 'There are lucky ones—those whose ticket to stardom gets drawn, whose YouTube clip goes viral, whose novel becomes a movie, whose phone App is snapped up. The winners get to live the dream. The rest of us hard-working sods settle for the crumbs; forced to find reward from our mediocre existence.'

'I see.' He grinned. 'And here's me thinking we make our own luck —once we stop being afraid of what might go wrong and get excited about what can go right. Positive people attract positive outcomes.'

Sally's shoulders sagged. 'Well, I've never even won a meat tray at the pub. Nothing ever goes right for me and this assignment is the perfect example. It could've been my big break. Instead, I'm stuck here with you.' The words were out before she could stop them. Harsh, unkind words very unlike Sally. 'I'm so sorry. That came out wrong.'

'What do you mean by "big break"?' he asked.

Sally huffed. 'Tomorrow's rally at the AGM should be Chase Storey's report. The Network's golden-haired boy gets to cover all the high-profile or controversial issues. He didn't need to go out of his way to impress them by going outside the brief. No wading shin-deep into a river for a headline shot. No, no, no! Chase Storey would've schmoozed up to those mine minders and scored an up close and personal with the CEO. Job done! Lead story on the nightly news! Happy producer! Big slap on the back and bigger bonus.'

A drawn-out pause followed, as if the guy was trying to comprehend. Eventually, he looked up at her. 'Maybe this Chase fellow reneged on purpose.'

'He didn't,' Sally answered. 'The Tasmanian bush fires have him stranded. No planes taking off until further notice.'

'And you got the gig by default.'

Sally nodded. 'Last flight out of Sydney, a couple of hours sleep and a hire car later, Liam and I arrive in Sunflower ready to kick butt —until karma kicked my cockiness away.'

'Rally's not until tomorrow and, unlike your colleague, you *are* at least in the same town. You're already way ahead in the game.'

'Journalism is no game,' she said, haughtily. 'But you're right. I am here, and Chase is the first one to say, "Reporting the news is all about right place, right time". But what a dork! That smarmy wink and phony voice at the end of every report drives me nuts.' Sally cupped an ear and forcing her voice unnaturally low said, '"This is Chase Storey, and I'm here chasing the big stories for *you*!" *Argh!*' She bent over, pretending to stick a finger down her throat. 'Doesn't that make you want to gag every time you hear him? You have heard him, right?'

'I don't bother with the news,' he told her. 'No television.'

'Oh, then you won't miss the Sally O'Neill report I won't be filing because I'm stuck soaking wet and stranded on some kind of weird island. Come to think of it ....' She stood before venturing down the front steps where she squinted through the thick stand of gumtrees. 'Tell me how it's possible to be surrounded by water in the middle of the outback?'

As she turned to look at him, the dimple in the man's chin twitched and his lips curled into a smile. 'Sunflower is not quite the outback. Just one of many small towns scattered across regional Australia.'

'And with no actual sunflower fields! Why is that?' she asked, stepping forward to finger the delicate, red grevillea flower.

When rustling sounds in the bushes moved Sally swiftly to the safety of the veranda steps, something huge and reptilian—but with legs, thank goodness—scurried away.

'Goanna,' he told her, 'They like it under the house. But there'll be snakes and spiders and insects all seeking dry ground. Most in the animal kingdom are sensible enough to stay out of floodwaters.' His grin grew so wide, the cleft all but disappeared. 'And if it helps, the water level will subside almost as fast as it rose. We only have to sit here and let Mother Nature do the work.'

Despite the snakes, the spiders, and her sodden clothing, Sally felt uncharacteristically upbeat. Usually when things went wrong at work, she would take her muted sobs and tears of frustration into a toilet stall. Or she'd head to the staff canteen in search of both comfort food and validation from other disheartened and peeved station personnel who felt similarly undervalued. But here, exposed to the elements and in the company of a curious stranger—a scenario that should unnerve her—Sally was invigorated. She leaned back on her hands, stretched her legs and closed her eyes. Perhaps more assignments in out-of-the-way country towns might help reclaim her missing mojo. She could think clearly and breathe clear air, and when she tipped her face towards the sun, a weird sensation—a kind of tingle—shivered her neck and travelled all the way to …

'My toes!'

As the startled goat stopped licking her pink nail polish and bleated in a murderous shriek, Sally's loud, pressure-releasing guffaw felt like the lid coming off a lemonade bottle. 'Oh, my giddy aunt!' She dabbed the corners of both eyes to head off any running mascara. 'No one at the Network will believe this story when I return to the office. *If* I return,' she added. 'If the SES crew haven't forgotten me?'

'I doubt you're easy to forget,' he remarked.

Suddenly self-conscious about her makeup, the wet jeans and still-sticky shirt, Sally sat up and hugged her knees to her chest. 'Here's me assuming I'd get at least one shot of the elusive Mr Garnet; a name clearly as fake and convenient as Chase Storey's sign-off.'

'You only want a photograph?'

'No,' Sally corrected, swivelling around to let him see she was serious. 'The plan is lots of photos. I mean, it's the pictures that add credibility, you know. They enhance the story, they bring context. Answers might also be nice. And, call me optimistic,' she added, 'but I prepared questions on the plane. I wrote them in my notebook.' Instinctively, she pressed a palm to her empty back pocket. *Great!* The notebook was gone. She scanned the expanse of murky water and exhaled loudly. 'With my luck, the closest thing I'll get is a shot of Garnet stepping off his private jet in his crocodile moccasins and Armani suit, which the editor might flick to one of our tabloid magazine affiliates.'

'You like Armani?' he asked.

What a peculiar question, Sally thought, observing his mousey-brown bun and the dried mud splatter on his spectacles.

'I said he'd be wearing it; not that I liked it,' she explained. 'Although, given the funds, I'm sure I'd learn to love Armani, a private jet, and three floors of a penthouse apartment. Wouldn't you?'

'Love it?' he sought to clarify. 'No. This, right here, is more my style.'

Sally was warming to the stranger, even though his preferred abode was a crooked little cabin in the middle of nowhere, and his only company assorted wildlife and a toenail-licking goat. At least he was honest—a trait Sally experienced less and less in a profession rife with fake news and unreliable sources. As if the biz wasn't disparaged enough, only last month the newly appointed Network News Director had hung his credo on the wall behind his desk: *The truth doesn't get ratings. Being first does.*

A cold was the only thing Sally would get if she stayed any longer in wet clothes. While the sun remained warm, the temperature at night would plummet, and at the rate things were going, her rescuers could make her wait that long.

'May I use your mobile?' she asked, plucking her own phone from a pocket. 'Mine is, well, as you can see …' The muddied device dangled between her thumb and index finger. 'At least the SIM card is salvageable.'

'I'm afraid I used the last of my battery to call the SES crew.'

Suspicion stiffened Sally's spine and her tone. 'No charger at all?'

'Well, yes, but a charger's not much use when a solar system is under water.' His finger indicated a point beyond the marooned rubber boat, now well clear of the subsiding waterline. 'I'm telling you the truth,' he added, as if reading her mind.

'So, you're not some weirdo hillbilly hippy hiding from the law?'

'Nope!' he said with a chuckle. 'But good on you for being curious but careful. Two admirable qualities, Sally. You're also wet, so this hillbilly best get a fire going. You could be waiting awhile. The only access for the crew is by water and your river adventure has left them down a dinghy.'

'I'll be fine outside in the sun,' she said, unwittingly rubbing her goosebump-prickled arms.

'I understand, but while it's no luxury penthouse, the cabin is comfortable and safe,' he said, standing. 'I'll put a fresh towel on the bed and find you something to wear. No Armani, but dry,' he said with a grin. 'Please come in, make yourself at home, get dry. Or stay in wet clothes if you prefer. Your choice, Sally. And should you change your mind, leave your muddy shoes on the rack, turn right inside the door, and you'll see the en suite bathroom. In the meantime,' he said while he made for the front door, 'I'll rustle up something to eat. I have a refrigerator full of food that'll spoil if we don't get it eaten.'

The offer of food set Sally's stomach rumbling and swayed her decision, as did the cool breeze whipping across the veranda.

After gathering her wet clothes, she stopped in front of the bathroom mirror, to check she looked decent in the oversized shirt and to ask herself two questions: Why was she feeling so unsure of herself? And when did they start making men's shirts so short? Her self-consciousness intensified when she tiptoed barefooted into the living area and the man's attention shifted from chopping cheese to eyeing her in a sweet looking-without-looking fashion.

'Have you lived in this place long?' she asked while draping her jeans and shirt over a makeshift clothes rack made from two stools.

'Long enough to know I want to be here more than anywhere else.' His focus returned to dicing cheese into small cubes. 'Sunflower has always been home. And living so close to nature brings special rewards and surprises.'

'Yes,' Sally chuckled. 'I met one of your surprises.'

'Giddy,' he said. 'Her name is Giddy and she's more entertaining than a cat. One minute she's reminding me to laugh and the next she's settled at my feet like a dog. That's what we do out here. We sit and contemplate. There's a quiet about the country, unlike any other place I've lived. I can breathe here.'

Breathe, that's it. Yes, Sally silently agreed.

'On the downside,' he added, breaking the spell, 'with no power, semi-warm beer is all I can offer.' He held the stubbie out as she settled on a stool opposite the kitchen counter and away from the fireplace that was quickly making the interior even cosier. 'Or how about H2O straight from the heavens?' He nudged a jug across the counter towards her, his grin adding even more warmth to Sally's cheeks. 'Unless you've had enough water for one day.'

'Ha! Water in a glass I can manage. Thanks.' Then, feeling cocky, she said, 'If you're so familiar with this town, you must have some goss on Ruby Garnet Mines.'

The man's initial reaction suggested he knew something, but he regrouped before Sally could interrogate further.

'I can tell you this,' he offered, as the last square of cheese landed on the plate. 'When you do your research you'll discover, unlike your Chase Storey nemesis, the CEO's name is genuine. Only Garnet is not pronounced gar-*net*, like the gemstone. The 'et' part is soft, as in Garn-*ay*.'

'Oh, I didn't know. Thanks.' Sally genuinely appreciated the heads-up. Imagine the embarrassment of filing a story with the incorrect pronunciation. They let talented journalists go for less. 'I'll lock the correct pronunciation into my brain.'

'Think Monet and ballet,' he suggested.

Sally kept the grin behind tight lips as she sipped more water. What experience did this cool-headed hick have with either of those things when his cabin walls were bare and painted beige? The sole two-seater sofa looked lumpy and worn on one side only, while a lone dining chair sat at a chunky wooden table.

The kitchen bench where Sally rested her folded arms was home to a typical masculine mess of paraphernalia, all pushed to one side rather than picked up and put away.

Looking from the food to the man's face she tried again. 'So, do you have any goss?'

'There is an interesting story few people have heard about the Garnet family.'

'Great! I'll take whatever you've got.' Again, Sally reached for the notepad and pen in the pocket of her pants and remembered. 'Damn!' Even if they'd survived the watery dunking, neither would be good for the job.

'Use these.' When he slid the substitute tools of her trade from the messy end of the bench and across the counter towards her, she tried not to smile at the shabby bundle of recycled paper torn into small squares and bound by string at one corner. 'I'm thinking we might need to sit outside while your clothes bake dry in here. What do you think?' he asked, sprinkling crackers to finish the cheese plate.

'Yes, please,' said Sally, plucking at the neckline of the shirt before taking charge of their drinks and heading for the door.

As the flyscreen snapped shut, a tiding of magpies tottered as if wearing vertiginous heels. The black and white birds abandoned the leaf matter left behind by the receding waters in favour of whatever was in the recycled margarine tub on the top step of the veranda.

'Will you tell me your story now,' Sally asked as she settled into the cane rocking chair to observe the gentle man crouched on the top step, hand extended and bird whistle tuneful.

'Where to start?' he muttered, as if to himself. Then, he shifted into a seated position, his back leaning against a post, one knee bent, gaze lowered, mien pensive. 'So … the Garnets,' he began, tossing the birds a worm-like treat. 'The family originated from England. Garnet's great-grandfather, Clem, escaped war-torn London as a small boy and he travelled to Australia with his older sister, Ruby. She, sadly, disappeared during the voyage. And, well, the rest of the family died during the Blitz… London Blitz.'

'So, Clem was a young orphan in a new country surrounded by water and miles from anything familiar?'

'An immigrant,' he went on, 'fostered out to a family by the Australian Government. All the ten-year-old knew was his name.'

'Where did the boy end up?'

'His first stop was Lakes Entrance, Victoria, where he waited and waited to be reunited with his sister.'

'They found her?'

'No.' He patted the lid back onto the tub. Treat time over. 'But Clem remained convinced she was wandering the ship's decks in search of him. He promised he'd find her, as soon as he was old enough.'

'But he didn't?'

'No. But around age fifteen, after several more foster homes, Clem saw a newspaper headline—"Garnets Found in Sunflower". The boy wasn't a good reader, and the town name was a confusing one—still can be,' he added with a smile. 'But Clem recognised his family name … Next thing he's on the road, stowing aboard trains, sleeping rough, and helped by outlaws and gangs who took pity on him.'

'But the article was referring to garn-*ets* being found—as in the gemstones?' The irony saddened Sally. 'Are you hoping I'll feel sorry for this young Garnet guy and in turn, the CEO who's his what? His great-grandson?'

'I doubt Clem was the kind to want pity,' he replied. 'But do you feel sorry for him?'

Sally scoffs. 'The guy's great-grandson ends up with three floors of penthouse. Should I?'

'That's harsh,' he tut-tuts, his green eyes narrowed and piercing. 'You judge a man on what he has, rather than on what he's achieved?'

'No, no, I-I'm just saying …' Was she judging? Had her job made her so cynical? 'Well, what I mean is we all have our sad stories.'

'And what's yours, Sally O'Neill, Intrepid Reporter?'

As quick as a wink, as he uttered the last word, she regrouped. She'd already shared too much about herself with this increasingly charismatic stranger. 'Let's stick with Clem's life, shall we?' Leaning forward in the rocker, she laced her fingers, propped her chin on her hands, and let her elbows dig into her knees. 'Tell me what happened to the boy. He made it to Sunflower?'

He nodded. 'It was the mid-fifties when the local mine operator gave the kid a break, a job, and a place to live. Clem repaid him by working hard—harder than anyone—and he grew into a fine man, gained respect, got promoted, and the mining family became his family.'

'And then?' Sally prodded when his storytelling stalled and he seemed to drift someplace else.

'Well, Clem married a local girl who bore him a son—John. Clem continued to work his way up through the company before establishing his own operation and calling it Ruby Garnet Mines, in memory of his sister. He sure had humble beginnings, but old Clem ended up leaving quite a legacy to his only son, who married in the early eighties and had a boy of his own—John Jnr.'

'As in the current CEO.' Sally knew that much. 'And it's John Jnr who's responsible for the mine today being global leaders in the production of industrial garnets for blast cleaning and water jet cutting?'

His eyebrows arched in surprise. 'You have done your research.'

'That's how I know shareholders aren't happy about a new investment,' she said, smugly.

'Only half of them,' he countered. 'An equal split, you said before—if I heard right.'

Rather than respond, Sally stood to stretch her legs. She wandered the length of the veranda while fidgeting with the cutaway shirt tail riding too high over her hips, and stopped by a table. Pretending to thumb the stack of tatty magazines, she stole several glances as the man hand-fed biscuit crumbs. One bird remained on high alert, serenading them from a nearby tree.

'I don't believe you've told me your name yet,' she said.

'Locals call me Digger.'

'Digger?' She poked her finger around the bowl of rocks sitting atop a stack of *Australian Prospecting & Fossicking* magazines. 'So, these rocks are what?'

'Green garnets in their raw state,' he answered. 'A friend sent those rare samples. In this country, most stones have a mulberry tinge.'

'I'm not familiar with garnets at all, other than they're pretty when they're polished and set in gold.' Sally examined her own hands, void of rings, except her right pinky that bore a signet ring embedded with a tiny, red stone in one corner. A twelfth birthday present from her Dad.

'Garnets are tough,' Digger said, 'and they're versatile. In fact, they're the hardest and toughest of natural minerals on the planet.'

'Excellent qualities for a gemstone, I guess,' Sally said while wishing he'd get back to Clem's story.

'Even better, the garnet symbolises patience and constancy,' Digger continued. 'Some will tell you they help us develop love and compassion.'

'Wow! Such a big burden for a simple stone.'

'You're welcome to take one. Plenty where they came from.' He nodded at the bowl. 'Grasp it tight when you need to calm your anger. Even the kind you direct at yourself.'

As her hand tightened and her gaze locked onto his, she realised the green in the stone was almost the same green in his eyes. 'Never picked you as a mystical, healing kind of guy. Then again, I didn't realise garnets could be green.'

'Lots of things aren't what we first think,' he said.

Sally recognised a sermon when she heard the start of one—and knew how to ignore one. 'So, you find them the old-fashioned way? Surely you could find a heap more using monster machines.' *Maybe make enough money to slap a coat of fresh paint on the house*, she wanted to add.

'Fossicking is a simple enough hobby if you know how,' he replied. 'Once these waters subside, there'll be a few easy-to-get-to areas further along the creek bed. But gemstones can be elusive buggers. Fossickers get used to coming home with empty pockets.'

'And yet you still do it? You waste hours searching by hand for things you may never find?'

'Whether I find anything isn't why I fossick,' he stated matter-of-factly. 'The process is therapeutic. Mother Nature provides ways for us to chill out. Here! Catch!'

Sally interpreted the cracker he tossed her way as an invitation to join the bird-feeding ritual from the top step. Within seconds she was clucking and nattering and shutting out the chaos of her life back in the city: the overpriced rental she shared with a messy stranger; the crowded commute; the street litter and graffiti. Then there was the loudmouth lout in the upstairs apartment who played his doof-doof music late into the night. No amount of bashing on the ceiling helped. The other ceiling Sally dealt with, despite working harder than most, was the impenetrable glass one at work. Advancement these days was very different to when the mine had rewarded a hard-working young Clem. Or, was the issue in Sally's case more about being judged by her gender rather than her achievements?

'Oh dear!' A thought came to her. What had Digger said earlier about her judging a man on where he lived and what he wore, rather than on what he'd achieved? Wasn't she guilty of the same? 'I think maybe I can add short-sightedness and cynicism to my list of failings,' she admitted.

'We can all do with broadening our horizons every now and then,' Digger said with a grin. 'If you don't stop the world and get off for a rest and a look around, you'll never realise when you stumble across something you want.'

She sighed. 'That's my problem. I no longer know what I want.'

'You're not enjoying your job?'

She paused to think before shrugging and twirling the signet ring on her little finger. 'I wanted to be a reporter like my Dad; he was everything to me, my rock, my moral compass. So, while other kids were singing into their hairbrushes and dreaming of fame, I was playing make-believe newsreader in the bedroom mirror. When Dad died, a month after my twenty-first birthday …' Sally's gaze followed the magpies as one by one they took refuge in a tree. 'I'd already absorbed his passion for journalism. I imagined being the teller of truths for my generation, like he was … but times have changed.'

'Changed how?' he asked.

'We have so many different ways of getting information these days and yet we're all so easily influenced, ill-informed, and quick to judge. Even me, it seems,' she added, coyly. 'The scourge of social media and fake news is destroying what was once a respected and responsible role, and it's not what Dad would have wanted for me.' Sally turned back and looked at Digger, raising her hands, fingers outstretched in declaration. 'And yet here I am!'

'Nothing makes a father prouder than a child following in his footsteps,' Digger said. 'You seem committed to your profession, but you're also right about changing times. We have no choice but to move with them and find ways around the bits we don't like.'

'Easier said than done,' she replied. Just talking about her job was sucking the joy from the moment. 'I should check my clothes.'

The fire had done its job. Though they were still slightly damp, Sally was instantly more comfortable in her jeans and top. If only her phone was as easy to remedy, she mused as she stepped back onto the veranda. The screen illuminated, but network reception was zero and the sun was getting low in the sky. Soon it would be dark. What then?

And why was she not freaking out and headed for the nearest toilet cubical for a meltdown?

'Sally?' Digger said from the same spot on the veranda step. 'I asked if you miss the sound of your ringtone?'

'Honestly?' Sally answered without hesitation. 'No. I'm even starting to understand why you live in the middle of nowhere.'

'It only looks like the middle of nowhere,' he said. 'The joy of a small town is in its roots. The tinier the town, the deeper you need to look. Maybe you'll drop by again before leaving for the city. I can show you the place through local eyes.'

'You forget,' Sally said, knowing she had as much chance of seeing Digger again as scoring her AGM exclusive and Chase Storey's salary package. 'As lovely as Sunflower sounds, this isn't a holiday. I'm here on an assignment. I must get back to the office—and with a photograph at least.'

'Oh, yes, the elusive CEO and tomorrow's rally. How could I forget?'

'But only if the SES come and get me.' Maybe, she thought, stepping off the veranda to survey the substantial water subsidence, the crew was waiting to drive in and collect her. 'You know the worst part about all this today, Digger?' As Sally ground a foot into the earth, the cool dampness on her soles squished between her toes, obliterating the fuchsia-pink polish. 'The girls in the office will never believe this story when I tell them.'

'I have an idea.' Digger stood and brushed the cracker crumbs from his palms, extending a hand to her. 'Let me see if the camera on your phone still works.'

'Why?' she asked, handing him the device.

'You said it yourself. A reporter needs images to add credibility to their story. Let's take some to show those girls.'

'Err, I suppose …' Sally agreed. 'At least they won't think I fabricated my rescue by a mysterious and handsome stranger.' *Oh my God!* Did she just say that aloud? 'Um, ahh, what I meant to say was—'

'Come on, then.' Digger was already backing away and lining up his shot.

'Hey, no, a location shot, not me. I'm a mess.' She darted to one side, fussed with her hair, and checked the buttons on her shirt.

'But we need context,' he wisecracked.

'Oh, you're hilarious, Digger. Have you even worked a phone camera?' Different to a flip-phone, she wanted to add.

'Reckon I can figure one out,' he replied. 'Let's get a shot of the rescue dinghy first.'

Through the cool shade of the same stand of trees she followed him, until they reached the rubber craft now sitting high and dry in the dying rays of sunlight.

'Oh, my Network press pass,' she announced as he collected the lanyard from the floor of the craft. 'Thanks.' But when she reached out her hand, he snatched the possession back and stared at the laminated ID featuring her name and the photograph of a visibly excited employee with big dreams and high hopes.

'This is you? Sallayla O'Neill?'

'Um, yeah, family name,' she explained. 'Grandma was born in Turkey and Dad's great-granddad was Irish. I grew up in Australia and, to be honest, in my line of work, Sally is easier.'

'Easier for who?'

'I'm not ashamed of the name, or my heritage, if that's what you're thinking. Friends outside of work call me Sallayla and I have lots of family who do the same. It's just, well, foreign-sounding names these days make people nervous. They tend to judge. You know? Like I'm not one of the good guys,' she clarified.

'Sallayla,' he said, softly. 'It's beautiful.'

When all Sally could do was blush and shrug and act like a silly teenager, Digger cupped a hand to his ear, mimicking her Chase Storey impersonation from earlier. 'Sallayla O'Neill,' he announced, 'bringing serious stories with heart and soul to *you!*'

'I reckon my Dad would like that.' Her blush intensified in heat, her cheeks burning to dry any trace of tears she might have cried as she shook away her melancholia. 'I don't suppose my notebook is in here anywhere.'

As she sat on the edge of the little boat to look, Digger snapped a photo. When she protested, he snapped another. Before she knew it, Sally was striking pose after pose, adding more theatre than necessary to her dramatic dinghy re-enactment until she and Digger were laughing too hard to continue.

'Okay, your turn, hero rescuer. Quickly, while we still have enough light.' Taking control, Sally flipped the camera and pulled Digger selfie-close. *Snap!* When he draped his arm around her shoulders for a second shot and squeezed tight to fit both their faces in the frame she realised what her life was missing was not a better salary package. It was a better connection.

Any connection! And laughter. Lots and lots of laughter, Sally.

'Ah, at last,' Digger said, pointing at a small tin boat motoring downstream. 'Look! There's your genuine flood hero.'

'Oh!' The word barely sounded in Sally's ears, drowned out by the drumming of disappointment in her chest. With her so-called knight-in-shining-dinghy bearing down too fast, not only was her departure imminent, Sally would soon be back to the hustle and bustle of a career encrusting her with scepticism. 'Digger?' she said, no longer rejoicing in her rescue. 'Please, I … I'm not ready for reality. I have to tell you.'

His brow creased into a million questions. 'What?'

She shook her head in disbelief. 'This makes no sense to me, which means I'm certain it won't make sense to you, but here goes.' Standing before him, shoulders squared and taught, chin high, she drew a deep breath. 'The SES might be rescuing me, Digger, but today—being here with you—has saved me in a way I could never have … never have …. Well, before I go, I'm thinking a thank you is in order.'

With his expression a clash of curiosity and amusement, he ignored the businesslike hand she extended, and leaned close until his face was very close to hers. 'And I'm thinking a kiss is in order, Sallayla O'Neill—if that's okay?'

As he lifted her chin, she whispered, 'Only if I can kiss you back.'

Sally recognised the SES Commander as he leapt from the tin boat, towline grasped in one hand. While sprouting apologies and reasons for the delay, he busily fixed the rubber craft to the rear of the metal dinghy and, after a brief and private exchange with Digger, and some notetaking, he urged Sally—now wrapped tight in a thermal emergency blanket—into the boat. Despite her loud pleas of 'I'm fine! I'm fine!' and her silent plea of *Let me stay. Let me stay*, daylight was fading fast.

'Here, Sallayla, take this with you.' Digger handed a folded scrap of paper to her, and their fingers touched. 'Remember,' he said. 'Be the person *you* want to be; not what others expect. Let them see Sallayla O'Neill's heart and soul in every story.'

As the rescue boat motored away from the island, the commander yelled over the engine noise. 'Don't worry, Miss, we'll have you home in no time.' He jerked his chin towards Digger and his little island. 'Nice, down-to-earth bloke, that John Garnet.'

'What?' Sally swivelled back around to stare at the distant figure, then down at the slip of paper she unfolded and read: *Please ensure the bearer of this note, Ms Sally O'Neill, has full press privileges at the AGM.* He'd signed the note: *John Garnet Jnr.*

Sally's hearty, belly laugh drew a curious glance from the man steering the boat. What had she said earlier about having as much chance of seeing Digger again as scoring her AGM exclusive?

Twice she'd been swept away today; Intrepid Reporter, Sallayla O'Neill, couldn't wait to see what happened next.

A PENNY FOR YOUR THOUGHTS

'Penelope, wait!' Determination edged his voice up a notch. 'Please don't close the door.'

'Who told you where I live, Cliff?'

He could have stuck with something vague. A cliché about how hard it is to hide in a small town like Sunflower. Instead, Cliff told the truth. Cliff always tells the truth.

'I asked Holly in Accounts, who checked with Molly in Payroll, who looked up your file and—'

'Why, Cliff?' she asked matter-of-factly. 'Why go to so much trouble when you can simply hack into the payroll database yourself? That is what your kind does, isn't it?'

My kind? Cliff queried silently, his stance stiffening. 'I don't *hack*.'

He wedged both hands into the front pockets of his jeans and loose change jangled with the sharp intrusion. One coin with a jagged edge had a distinctive shape and size, as though it wanted to stand out from the rest. Maybe that was the connection he'd felt as his hand had fisted around the discovery. Trying to stand out was the story of Cliff's life.

Pinching the battered coin between his thumb and index finger, Cliff wished he'd found a magic lamp in the car park today. He could do with three wishes right now. He'd settle for one—a chance to implement Plan B because Plan A with Penelope was not getting off to a good start.

If only she'd worked back, as usual. He would have passed by her desk, casually struck up a conversation, asked her to have a drink. Or a glass of courage, as Cliff called that first beer on any first date. Instead, Penelope had left work angry—with him, according to the office scuttlebutt—and Cliff had to know why. So here he was at her door rather than the local pub, sober and struggling for words.

For weeks he'd rehearsed the conversation starter. *So, Penelope*, he planned to start. *Do you believe in love at first sight?* In the event she laughed, Cliff intended blaming the beer and a bad day before fabricating a story about asking for a friend—a non-existent mate who'd fallen hard. But Penelope's premature departure from work today had put a gaping hole in his strategy and in his self-confidence. That was until his find in the office car park. The battered coin had decided for him. *Heads!*

He'd pocketed the coin, telling himself, *Find a penny, pick it up, and all the day you'll have good luck.* That luck, however, seemed to wane under the weight of Penelope's next statement.

'Well, Clifford Garnet, whatever you have to say, you'll need to hold off until tomorrow at work. I'm busy.'

'It can't wait. I can't wait,' he blurted. 'I'm here. You're here. We need to talk.'

Despite sounding a tad crazy, perhaps a little desperate, he knew this was his now-or-never moment. The trouble was, words didn't come easily for computer nerds like Cliff, who communicated in code five days out of every week.

Standing on Penelope's welcome mat and observing her unwelcoming gaze, Cliff struggled to utter a coherent sentence. 'Can I, um, come in, or, ah, do I … um, say what I came to say out here on the front porch?'

If there were unshed tears behind Penelope's eyes—leftovers from her afternoon misery-fest—Clifford Garnet's earnest expression siphoned them away. He was the last person she expected to see at her screen door. Seeing his face on the other side of her desk every day was difficult enough.

Ever since the new IT expert arrived from the city, Cliff had been the butt of office jokes, although never to his face; not with his grandfather and father both Ruby Garnet Mining Corporation board members.

Penelope might have felt sorry for the guy; she also might have stood up for him in the staffroom this morning when the jokes had started, but she'd been too busy being angry. Even if her anger was misplaced; it wasn't Clifford's fault his family owned the mega corporation. Without the Garnet mine operation, Sunflower would struggle to survive. The Garnets all but owned Penelope's home town.

Still, some older locals harboured resentment, and recent retrenchment rumours were fuelling office gossip more than usual—the air tense, tempers tested. Discovering Clifford's plans to sack her had not only left Penelope on a slow simmer all day; they'd stirred decade-old memories of her Dad; pain which still burned deep. Computerised tools introduced in the late 1980s had made Ted Miller redundant.

◡

'Bugger technology!' her father had said. More than once. He'd gaze out the window of his weatherboard cottage—inherited from his parents and lived in his entire life—and mutter. 'They reckon some gizmo and gadget can do the job better than a human. I wasn't needed, love. God-awful thing for a man to hear at my age.'

Penelope still recalled her mother sobbing at night in the weeks after his retrenchment; her strength each morning as she tried to motivate her husband. 'You are needed, Ted. We need you.' But the man who never complained, the night-shift worker who never took a sickie, was never the same again.

Within two years, Ted Miller was dead.

'I'm sorry, Clifford,' Penelope said, barely keeping it together. 'This isn't a good time.'

'Please, call me Cliff. Clifford is what my parents call me and reminds me of all the expectations being in the family brings.'

The jab at his family sparked Penelope's interest, the admission unexpected. She'd blamed Ruby Garnet Mining Corporation for breaking her father's heart. In truth, his death was nothing to do with the company and everything to do with the tumour that had silently festered inside his body for years. And while the redundancy payout had helped the family and provided medical intervention to prolong his life, Penelope had gained something more precious than money.

From that moment, she didn't have to play silent games in the house after school or be constantly shushed so she didn't wake the man who worked all night and slept all day. Penelope got to know her dad; to know the warmth of his hug and the breadth of his love.

Three months earlier, in anticipation of a Y2K Millennium bug debacle, head office had dispatched Clifford to the Sunflower-based operation. Despite his flash office and the responsibility of upgrading the company's technology, the man spent a disproportionate part of his day hovering around the workers' cubicles. Never far from Penelope, always watching her with his alarmingly sweet smile and animated eyes, Clifford solved every computer problem. He taught shortcuts and shared his knowledge with the staff and, as recently as today when Penelope's computer had crashed, it was Mr Nice Guy Clifford who'd got her back online faster than she could repeat her father's words: *Bugger technology!*

Damn Clifford Garnet! she said to herself. As likeable as the guy might be, he was the IT Manager, and ten years ago a company IT manager had seen nothing wrong with replacing a dedicated team of process workers with new technology. If that wasn't reason enough to avoid Clifford, Penelope's silent stance against romantic involvements with fellow Ruby Garnet employees was—even if the self-imposed policy made for slim pickings around town. Penelope might be twenty-five and still single, but she wasn't so desperate for a date she'd go out with the man about to make her redundant.

An hour earlier she was telling herself redundancy was the best thing. A cash injection would let her get away from this town while she was still young. If only she didn't love Sunflower so much and see memories of her father everywhere in this house. What did it say about her that she was proud of the small-town girl label, happy to grow old in the place she and generations of family before her had lived? Surely leaving wasn't the only way to better oneself. No town would survive if their youth took off to the city after finishing school. Sunflower was vibrant today because generations of families like hers had stuck around. Generations had fought to ensure its future and sustainability despite industry gobbling all the goodness up.

Clifford Garnet and his redundancy package would not drive her away. That *was*, she assumed, the reason he was hovering on her front doorstep all squeaky clean and shower fresh. Far from the stylish upstart she saw in the office nine to five, this not-so-geeky alter ego in the black T-shirt, faded jeans, and RM Williams boots was unexpected and a tad unsettling—as were his wide, green eyes resplendent with flecks of amber. Or was it topaz?

Good grief, Penelope! Are you contemplating the colour of Clifford's eyes?

She fiddled with her wristwatch, unsure where to look or how to act. Aware Clifford was tall, she'd never realised how broad his shoulders were until framed by her front door. The outfit he wore might be casual, but he was carefully groomed, which made Penelope the frumpy geek of the moment.

Two hours earlier, she'd raced home and thrown on her oldest and most comfortable three-quarter-length pants and a pastel pink singlet top patterned with last night's pasta sauce and begun her frantic search. With her hair in a half-up, half-falling-down state of confusion, and her nose and eyes stinging from too many tears and tissue wipes, she looked like she'd spent two hours ferreting through every nook and cranny of her house and car.

Assuming the treasured possession was likely lost forever made her want to cry until something in the expression on her visitor's face suggested she wasn't the only stressed-out person. Cliff's glance at her midriff also let her know the drawstring on her pants had loosened, putting the waistband low over her hips and exposing the decorative ring in her belly button. If she turned her back on Clifford now, the butterfly tattoo and its large colourful wings on her lower back would, likewise, be on display without permission.

'Okay, well, you'd best come inside.' Penelope shoved the screen door wide open before stepping back. 'I gather you've come to my house to avoid making a scene at the office?'

The man flinched. Either the door snapping shut behind him, or the chaotic consequences of her room search spread out before him had stopped Clifford in his tracks. 'A scene?' he queried.

Refusing to crumble, Penelope breathed deep and prepared herself for the bad news. 'Go ahead. Get it done,' she said, ramming both her hands hard on her hips. 'Put me out of my misery.'

'Your misery?' Cliff's brow puckered until his eyebrows looked like bookends pushing against the three vertical creases in the middle of his forehead. 'I was hoping you'd put me out of mine.'

His words didn't compute. 'Sacking me is making *you* miserable?' she asked, incredulous.

'Sacking you would most definitely make me miserable, Penelope. Why would you think I was here to sack you? You're great. Management loves you and—'

'Hang on a minute, Cliff,' she interrupted. 'If I'm so great, why mark my desk space as a void?'

Cliff's hand went to his head, momentarily lifting his fringe. 'A what?'

'There was a note on your desk,' she explained, 'along with a plan for new workstations.'

He studied her. 'How do you know what's on my desk?'

Penelope's momentary panic shifted into a smug smile to match the smart-alec tone in her voice. 'Oh, you know how it is, Cliff.' She tipped a cocky head to one side. 'Holly from Accounts saw it and told Molly in Payroll who—'

'Okay, okay, point taken.' His arms folded in a Chesty Bond kind of way, his grin morphing from a nervous curve into a full and perfect smile. 'What exactly did this so-called note of mine say?'

With nothing about his tone or his expression fitting with the office gossip, a tremor threatened to dilute the determination in Penelope's voice, but she held firm. 'The note,' she said and lifted her chin in a challenge, 'had the words: Penelope Miller's desk —VOID.'

'Void?'

'Yes, Clifford, void!' Collecting cushions from the floor, she spelled the word. 'V–O–I–D.' Then, with each cushion she beat into the corner of the sofa, Penelope delivered the word's numerous definitions for the man's benefit. 'Void—as in an empty space.' *Thump!* 'As in cancelled.' *Thump!* 'Vacant, not occupied.' *Thump!* 'Need I go on?' She scanned the room for more cushions.

'No,' Cliff said. 'Because it's not void, Penelope. It's *V–o–I–P* with a 'P'. It stands for *Voice over Internet Protocol*.'

Penelope froze and mulled over his reply before muttering the term—'voip'—like testing out a new and naughty swear word. If only it was. She sure could do with one, because *bloody idiot* didn't seem nearly good enough. 'Are you for real, Cliff?'

'Yes,' he said, straight-faced. 'VoIP is a new system for a new century. It's really good news for those of us in regional business.' The man's eyes bugged with excitement. 'The company's bringing in the technology for the new Customer Care Division and, Penelope, we want you to manage the team of consultants. It's a promotion. You'll be in charge of the entire VoIP implementation. I fought to make it happen; not that it was hard to do. You've impressed management with your passion and how you live up to the little credo you've got stuck above your workstation.'

'What little credo?'

'You know, "There may be no 'i' in team",' Cliff recited, "but every successful team has a leader." You are our chosen VoIP leader, Penelope. You do your best every day.'

'I–I do? I, ah, I mean, yes, I sure do, Cliff. Of course. I love my job.'

'Great, because there'll be even more opportunities as we continue our expansion, unless …' Those worry lines wiggled back into place on his forehead. 'Do you have plans to leave, Penelope?'

'If you mean Sunflower, then no. I–I don't want to leave. I love this town, but…' The sofa provided a soft place to land. She hugged a cushion to her chest and pictured the creeping, neon-like blush on her neck. 'You mean I have a promotion and you came here to tell me?'

'Yes and no,' he said. 'I mean, the job is yours, if you want, but my visit is, umm … Well it's—' Uneasiness nudged its way back into his voice and eclipsed the earlier enthusiasm.

'Out with it, Cliff.' She insisted. 'Tell me why are you're here.'

'I, um, came over to get your thoughts on, um, a date.'

'A date? Oh, you mean for the implementation? You're worried about the January 1, 2000 thing, of course. I understand about the 2KY Millennium bug and the fact you want my input is, well, I'd be thrilled to—'

'No, you have it all wrong,' he interjected. 'The world will not end at midnight on December 31. A date like *that* I can handle,' he said, the words tumbling out on a nervous laugh. 'I mean going out on a date —with me.'

◡

When Penelope's teeth pinched her bottom lip, and she tipped her head to one side, eyes narrowing, Cliff hoped there wasn't meanness in her silence. The schoolboy with the bottle glasses had been no stranger to rejection; always the last one selected on team sports day. Labelled 'the boring, brainy type' by kids in his class, not a lot had changed, with some grown women just as quick to write off a matured Cliff without a second glance. He might not be stud material, but he wasn't a total nerd. Some people just didn't give him a chance to show them. He hoped the woman sitting on the sofa in front of him, eyes misting over from an obvious maelstrom of emotions, was not one of those unkind people. But with her silence more nail-biting than a network crash, and more stomach-churning than a computer's blue screen of death, Cliff knew only one thing.

He'd known the moment Penelope had answered the door with the red nose and puffy eyes. *Cliff, mate, your timing sucks!* Idiot, he cursed. Good timing was everything when one planned to rip one's chest open and lay one's heart on one's sleeve. More than anything, as he stood there, the little coin clenched in the fist hanging by his side, Cliff wished he could read her thoughts.

The only thing banging against Penelope's brain was how silly she must seem to Clifford Garnet. She'd let herself get into a terrible state, searching everywhere conceivable for her father's lucky penny, going over the same spots multiple times. Mentally, she was still turning the room upside down. Anything to avoid the man and his question.

'Sorry, Cliff, I'm sorta searching for something and I'm not having much luck.'

He smiled, his gaze skimming the area over her right shoulder. 'I can sorta tell.'

'The thing is, Cliff, I'm feeling ridiculously sad and angry with myself for losing it.'

'Must be important,' he said, his smile—perceptive rather than patronising—calmed Penelope.

'My father's lucky coin,' she explained. 'He found it on the day he and Mum married. Nine months later I came along, which is how I got my name. He and Mum called it a destiny penny. Somehow, I've stupidly lost it between here and work. I can't believe it.' Mortified as one of those unshed tears spilled over, Penelope lowered her gaze before swiping at her cheek with the heel of a hand. *Why was the man not saying anything?* 'I'm an idiot,' she blurted. 'The coin is always tucked in the little pocket section of my handbag. Always!'

Still the man stood in exasperating silence, his head cocked in a curious tilt, his hand extended towards Penelope, the closed fist palm up.

Then, unfurling one finger at a time, Cliff said, 'You can't mean this, can you?'

Clutching two hands to her chest, not daring to reach out in case the coin vanished, she sat statue-still, eyes blinking in disbelief. 'My penny! But ... Where? How?'

'In the gutter by my car and caught up in leaves. It looked ragged, really old and I thought it's possibly worthless, but I picked it up anyway. You know ... *Find a penny, pick it up ...* I knew I'd need luck if I came here today.'

'Luck?' Penelope stood and edged forward; her eyes glued to the coin on Cliff's palm. As she reached out, Cliff closed his fist over the battered coin and drew his hand back and out of her reach.

'Not so fast,' he said through a smile. 'First, Ms Miller, a penny for your thoughts.'

Confusion forced a step back. She needed distance and perspective. She needed to think. 'Clifford Garnet, what are you doing? What's this about?'

'A confession,' he said. 'Two confessions actually: one, I've always wanted the opportunity to use that "Find a penny line" for real, and two, a few minutes ago I asked what you thought about going out on a date.' A step forward narrowed the space between them, and Cliff unfurled Penny's fingers and pressed the cherished currency into her palm. 'A date with me.'

'I see, well then.' Penelope stifled a grin and looked up, her eyes locking on his—big and green. *And, yes, definitely topaz.* 'Maybe we can see in the Year 2000 together after all.' She held her palm with the penny out towards Cliff. 'But first, it's my turn. A penny for *your* thoughts, Cliff Garnet.'

He cupped Penelope's hand between both his and deliberately curled her fingers closed to encase the coin. 'This afternoon I thought this penny might bring me luck. Now I'm kind of hoping your Dad was right, and it is a destiny penny.'

Penelope grinned. 'I look forward to finding out.

GERONIMO

I was thirty-eight when I jumped. Not what I called a brave decision at the time. I'd never considered myself brave. Even the note I left behind had screamed 'coward' and lacked both compassion and content. But there was nothing left to say; between us we'd shouted every mean and hurtful accusation during each fight over our ten years together.

Quick was easy.

Brief was best.

A single word more than enough.

My word inspiration came from a story my late father once told me about the courageous US Army's parachute test platoon at Fort Benning. In the early 1940s, on the eve of their first jump, the men had watched an old Western featuring a brave Native American Indian chief named Geronimo. Little did I realise, however, I would one day leap out of my marriage and into the unknown, and those paratroopers and their ritual would provide me with the perfect farewell letter to Brad. That single word.

Geronimo.

Where did that recollection come from after all these years?

Is it because I'm trapped on a plane the size of an insect and wondering where the pilot has stowed the parachutes? Or has my destination triggered the memory? The school reunion has been twenty years in the making according to the 1988 Student Yearbook I clutch on my lap, because it wouldn't fit in the cabin bag.

Why are you doing this, Grayce? You hate flying more than you hate the school reunion concept. And why has the undersized aircraft not yet moved?

The propellers are spinning. I can see them from my window seat. The spinning blades have all my attention and they mimic a mind whirling with the endless array of disastrous school reunion scenarios. My palms are sweaty, my stomach is home to a butterfly invasion, and both legs twitch uncontrollably under the very conservative and practical cotton skirt. Then, as the plane shudders and jerks into motion, I take a deep breath to slow my pounding heart.

As the Dash-8 aircraft flight crew finish the perfunctory safety-card-in-the-seat-pocket presentation, my thoughts shift to the stable job I've held for fifteen years, and the self-propagating stack of papers on my desk growing taller by the second. Both the pile and the plane will probably reach twenty-five thousand feet at the same time. Mentally pushing all work worries away I suck in my stomach, yank the seatbelt tighter and squeeze my eyes shut. I plan for them to remain so until I reach my destination; my home town of Sunflower.

'Coffee, tea, or … juice?' Although it's not quite the hackneyed line with the come-hither connotations from the eighties, the smiling hostess dispenses the words with the same portion-controlled sugariness, while her manicured fingers clutch two stainless steel jugs.

I sit straight, like a schoolgirl hoping good posture will help my cause, and clasp both hands on my knees. Then, impersonating Oliver's appeal for more porridge, I ask, 'Please, may I have something stronger? Gin and tonic perhaps? I have money.'

The woman is now unsmiling, her silent reprimand clear in a raised eyebrow. 'No alcohol on this flight, sorry.'

Why not? I want to probe. When did airlines stop serving drinks? I'd boarded my first small plane at eighteen, desperate to run away from home, from a badly broken heart, from small-town scrutiny, and from the syrupy commiserations of locals. There'd been booze on board back then.

What was the world coming to?

'Nothing hot for me, thanks.' I reposition the journal to my lap and idly turn pages.

'We have juice,' she announces. 'Unless you prefer water.'

On the tip of my tongue are the words *I'd prefer a G&T* but Water Woman's perfectly painted smile is already fading in frustration.

'No. Thanks anyway,' I tell her.

Bottled water—with or without the nip of annoyance and dash of disapproval in the crew member's voice—will never be a substitute for a nerve-numbing G&T. Bottled water won't help me survive a school reunion either, should the face staring back at me from the open yearbook on my lap make an appearance in person. *Parker Edwards!* The boy I would marry. The boy whose initials I'd carved into our tree in the playground. The boy who'd chosen Pamela, my best friend.

'Big reunion in town?'

I hear the voice beside me, but humiliation won't let me look up. My late and lubberly arrival, due to a bout of last-minute indecision at the boarding gate, had meant beating my cabin bag and coat into submission in the crowded overhead locker. I'd done so under the critical gaze of crew, and passengers in Rows 2 onwards, before slipping self-consciously into seat 1A, fully aware of seat 1B's undeniable disappointment at not scoring the coveted spare seat for the flight. I'd barely registered the passenger was male until he spoke and I turned my head to acknowledge his presence and to smile the required apology. At least the front row had let me avoid the embarrassing bum-in-the-face-squeeze-past to access my allocated seat.

'Yes,' I reply. 'Sunflower High, tonight.' I tug at the skirt still strangled under the tight seatbelt. 'Still not sure if I'll go.'

I sense 1B's body shift towards me and when I look, his brow is creased, his mouth turned up at the corners. 'You're on a plane, headed for a small-town school reunion you might not attend?'

'It's not as silly as it sounds. The flight cost me less than a hundred bucks, it's a little over an hour in the air, and I had nothing better planned for Saturday night. Come to think of it, I had nothing planned for a Friday night, either.'

'But you clearly don't like flying.'

'True!' I confess. 'What gave me away? The white knuckles or pleading for a G&T?'

He says nothing, letting the laugh lines on his middle-aged face, along with two straight rows of celebrity-white teeth, speak for him. While I try not to stare, his expression captivates me, his buttery voice calming.

'So, what takes a man like you to a small place like Sunflower?'

'The Speakers Bureau booked a gig for me,' he says. 'The Ruby Garnet Mine corporate powwow. I'm the entertainment.'

'Really?' A block of embarrassment lodges in my throat as I realise the teeth, the beautiful face, and the broad shoulders I'm rubbing against must belong to someone famous.

What a shame another stealthy sideways glance cannot solve the mystery. While infinite possibilities lurk behind those long, luscious lashes and the shiny, sculpted cheekbones, I rule out Hollywood megastar. The accent is too unmistakably Australian. Sports star, maybe? Hmm, with my luck he'll be a football player. I have little interest in the sport. I'm basically clueless about most codes. So, I ask.

'Given I'm not the sporty type, I'm afraid I ... Oh, what the hell!' I release the seat belt a tad to twist in my seat for a proper look and our eyes meet. 'I have to ask, because I feel like an idiot for not recognising you. I gather you're famous?'

'Not at all.' The man seems amused. 'You're not an idiot and I'm not famous. I'm a guest speaker who has a story to tell.'

'Ah, yes, I see.' I snuggle back into place alongside those strong shoulders and try to make out the embroidered emblem on the coat he's draped across his legs. 'You're one of those motivational gurus?'

He laughs. 'Not quite guru status, but I hope to educate people with my talk.'

'Educate them about what?'

'About taking risks,' he says.

'Oh, right, as in advising factory workers not to take them. Occupational health and safety stuff. I get it.'

'No, no, I motivate people from all walks and stages of life not to be afraid, and I explain that not all risk-taking ends badly.'

'Yeah right!' I huff and flap a dismissive hand. 'I don't do risky. Never have, never will.' *Unless you count walking away from a marriage and starting again,* she reminds herself, *and with nothing more than a Barbra Streisand record collection.* 'So then, I'm guessing you took risks, and you lived to tell the tale?'

A trace of amusement reaches the lips I can't stop looking at. 'Ditch the reunion and come with me as my guest tonight,' he says. 'You'll see and hear the story for yourself. I put on a good show.'

'I'm sure you do.' I cast seat 1B my biggest smile, realising I'm enjoying the flight, enjoying the banter, enjoying him. 'No doubt you're quite the song-and-dance man.'

'I can't promise dancing,' he says with a grin. 'But my talk does begin with the words of a song.'

'Something rousing like Jimmy Barnes' "Working Class Man" or are you a "Don't Worry, Be Happy" guy?'

When he laughs, his eyes light up. 'All great choices, but no. The song is titled "A Piece of Sky", and the lyrics speak about a life lived on the ground being safer, but sometimes the sweetest of pleasures come from taking risks and learning to fly.'

I recognise the song immediately. 'You. Know. Barbra? No way!' I gush.

'You. Know. *Yentl?*' He mimics.

'Know *Yentl?* Best movie ever. Oh my gosh! I love the messages, the soundtrack—everything. I can't believe you do.' Though eager to discover what else he and I might have in common, disappointment soon douses any delight. *Of course!* I mentally smack my palm on my forehead. *Just my luck. He's gay.*

'Your turn?' Seat 1B says, interrupting my thoughts.

'My turn what?'

'You love Streisand and a G&T, but you fear flying, hate sports, and avoid risks. Tell me more.'

I shake my head. 'My life isn't interesting enough to talk about.'

'I'm sure that's not true.'

'Oh, believe me. I've no reason to lie.' *And less reason to impress*, I remind myself, taking in the stylish attire, the ultra-clean shave, and the strong scent of hair product that when put together screams—

'Hey!' His shoulder nudges mine. 'Tell me the three things.'

'I-I, ah, beg your pardon?' I'm feeling immediately sprung when he holds up a fisted hand, sticks out his thumb and counts off with fingers.

'Relax, I'm only asking you to tell me three things you do every week. Only if you want to, of course. Just passing the time.'

'Oh!' I breathe. 'Sure, no problem at all. Too easy, in fact. I work. I work a lot.'

'And what drives you?' he asks.

I huff a laugh, the game getting easier. 'Charlie, from the bus company, drives me. A sweet Pakistani who smells of curry most mornings and sings Bollywood songs while behind the wheel. Next question?'

My girlish giggle mixes with 1B's warm, buttery laugh and I'm aware I should lower the laughter volume, but not only has my usual self-control gone AWOL, I'm feeling defiant and far less concerned about the censorious stewardess.

'Tell me this then,' he says. 'What makes you jump out of bed every morning and say, "I'm doing something today *just because*"?'

'Me? Jump? Ha!' My sass is short-lived as the reality of a small, safe existence sinks in. I have no stories to share with this stranger. I have no stories, full stop. 'There's not a brave or impulsive bone in my body,' I tell him. 'I'm a planner—except for today and I admit, far too little thought went into boarding this plane.'

His gaze homes in on me, both eyes an unfathomable azure abyss I would happily fall into. If only I took risks.

'The only bad plan is the one that stops you doing what you want,' he tells me. 'What's the worst thing going to your reunion might bring about?'

'Argh! Where to start? As a worst-case scenario girl I've planned for every possibility and every negative consequence.' What I don't tell him is contingency plans and conventionality have controlled every aspect of life, including my wedding day. Nor do I mention that the need to conform is what kept me clinging to the wrong man for too long. Not being brave, not having the mettle to go against the tide, is why there have been no *just because* moments. 'Do you want to understand why I'm going, or perhaps not going to this reunion tonight?' I ask while thumbing the pages of the book in my lap until I stop to tap three times on a face smiling back. 'This guy. Parker Edwards. I planned on marrying him.'

'Why didn't you?'

'He didn't pick me in the end.'

'Well, that there is one stupid guy. I assume he was a bit loopy?' With a finger pointed at the side of his head, he draws invisible circles while crossing his eyes. 'Who did he choose? Is she in your book? Show me.'

'Yes, she was my best friend at the time.' When I poke my painted nail at the photograph, he leans closer. 'Meet the teeny-weeny-waisted, big-breasted, boyfriend-pinching Pamela.'

'Will she be there tonight?' he asks. 'Is Pamela why you're not keen to go?'

I shrug. 'Not sure. Part of me hopes they've split up. Gosh!' I let the book drop to my lap before snapping the cover shut. 'I sound mean. It's not about wanting Parker—not then and not now. I'm all grown up—a divorced woman of two years with no plans and no desire to jump into another relationship.'

'Perhaps going will provide some closure,' he suggests.

'Closure?' I scoff. 'Aren't we the Dash 8 Dear Abby?' I nudge his solid shoulder with mine and we both laugh. 'How about you, Mr No-wedding ring? Got a wife? A girlfriend?' *A boyfriend?* I'm tempted to add.

'One wife,' he answers. 'Years ago.'

'A wife? Really? Well, that's good. I mean—'

His expression makes me think he's read my mind. 'There was a girlfriend until recently,' he says, 'and an engagement somewhere in the middle—shortest in history. I can't find a woman willing to take the risk.'

'I see, so is risk taker an essential quality?' The question is provocative for two strangers, but I'm feeling bold and a little mischievous. Must be the altitude. 'How brave do they need to be?' I enquire. 'Is scaling mountains required?'

'Taking risks in love is not about courage,' he says, stony-faced. 'It's about being decisive and willing to entrust our heart to someone else's care for eternity.'

I hear my gasp and a sudden lack of oxygen leaves me winded. Definitely the altitude, I tell myself as his words suck the last smart alec-speck from my body, daring me to rip open my chest right there and let him have all my heart. I don't, of course. I don't do crazy. I don't do spontaneous. I don't take risks. And I don't do things 'just because'.

The plane is banking and descending, taking my high spirits down with it. 'For so many reasons right now, I wish I was brave,' I say, staring at the clouds outside the window, regret grinding my voice flat. 'I'm not.'

'You're going to a twenty-year school reunion on your own. Sounds pretty plucky to me'.

'You mean pretty pathetic.'

The seatbelt light illuminates and after tucking the belt tight, my fingers clench the armrests. Head back, eyes closed, I brace against the seat and visualise a giant Gin & Tonic; the cool, clear courage in a glass providing a sense of calm. After a few seconds, I realise it's not the imagined alcohol soothing me at all. The calming elixir is his voice, and his hand clasping mine, comforting me, making me brave.

. . .

When the aircraft's wheels tease the tarmac, I open my eyes to find 1B staring.

'See, you are courageous,' he says.

'You and your repertoire of corny *Knock, Knock* jokes helped. Thanks.' I press the palms against my aching cheeks, struggling to recall when I'd last smiled so hard my face hurt. I can't.

Bing-bong! The aircraft's speaker system works like the clapper board on a movie set.

'Welcome to Sunflower,' a trained voice parrots. 'Please remain seated until the captain turns off the seatbelt sign and the aircraft has come to a complete stop at the terminal.'

Suddenly, I'm screaming inside. *No, no, don't stop! Take off again. Go around—again, and again, and again.* For the first time in my life I want to keep flying and forget about my job, the paperwork, the reunion, my very ordinary life.

Unfortunately, the plane does stop, the doors do open, and while the cabin lights flicker and passengers struggle with overhead lockers and bags, I wait in my seat. I am in no hurry and it seems neither is my neighbour.

'I'm Grayce, by the way. Grayce Lewis.'

'Zachary Dawson. Zac for short.'

Goodness! Even his name is beautiful.

'Nice to meet you, Zac.' I stall by rolling up the yearbook and forcing it to fit into my handbag, but the aircraft is emptying as quickly as my list of reasons to delay. 'Guess I need to grab my stuff and get going.'

'You first,' he says, adding *gentleman* to the catalogue of admirable Zachary Dawson qualities.

Moving into the aisle I reach into the overhead locker, aware my T-shirt is lifting, exposing my ten-tummy-tucks-a-day abs.

'Well, Zac.' I move to the front to let a final passenger pass and juggle the coat and bag in my left hand to extend my right arm. 'Thank you,' I say, but for what, I'm not sure.

'Grayce?' He's staring up from his seat, his eyes alive with a challenge. 'About going to the reunion ... Don't go.'

'What?' One syllable at a time is all my ricocheting brain can manage. 'Why not?'

'Just because,' he says, smiling.

Heat shoots through my body, lava-like blood searing every artery. 'Just because why?' I barely manage to ask him.

'Because I don't want you to be alone tonight, Grayce, especially with regret.'

'But I thought you said I was brave for taking a risk and going solo.'

'I'm still asking you to take a risk, Grayce, but with me.'

I draw a sharp breath. 'Wh–what?'

His grip tightens around my hand. 'Come to my talk. Do something spontaneous, *just because.*'

I notice Water Woman at the exit door glancing at her watch, her bogus smile urging me to hurry, but the thought of leaving, of peeling my hand away from his, almost hurts. So, I brace and think like a bandaid. The quicker it's done, the less painful the procedure.

'I've told you already, Zac, I don't do *just because* well. I am one hundred percent certain of that fact. What I can't tell you, however, is why I'm still standing here.' I snatch back my hand and close my fingers into a fist. Humour remains my only remaining defence so I laugh, but it's a strange, strangled sound. 'Usually, I won't get on a plane. Now it seems they can't get me off.'

'I'm glad you were on this plane. I enjoyed our time together,' he says. 'Please, make the most of tonight—and your life. You'll knock 'em dead at the reunion. I think you're amazing—*Grayce!*' He winks and I try not to laugh again, but it's impossible.

'I think, Zac Dawson, you are not overly original, because if only I got a dollar each time I heard that "Amazing Grace" line, I'd charter a plane.' The exaggerated roll of my eyes is subterfuge. I'm totally wired and his smiling face just lit the fuse. I picture the spark fizzing through my body, igniting every nerve as it travels from my head to my toes before finally blasting my defective feet into action. 'Okay, now the crew are giving me the death stare, Zac. I've got to go. Enjoy your gig at Ruby Garnet Mines. I hear they put on lots of booze.'

Before he can say anything else I charge from the plane and down the stairs to join the unruly line of meandering passengers heading for the terminal's baggage collection area.

I'm focused on the baggage cart en route from the plane when out of the corner of my eye an airport worker in a fluorescent safety vest steps into my peripheral vision. The man is opening the *Staff Only* access doors into the terminal for a passenger in a wheelchair.

'Hello again.' Zac Dawson propels himself to my side, finishing with a kind of wheelchair wheelie, while on the tarmac the baggage cart driver with Mario Andretti aspirations is doing a three-hundred-and-sixty-degree turn. The wheelchair stops; so, too, the cart. My brain does not. It's desperately replaying the last hour and fast-forwarding through every word, every throwaway line, every joke from our exchange on the plane. I pray my 'quite the song-and-dance man' comment has been the only in-flight faux pas.

How did I not notice?

Zac flicks his head toward the airport worker in the green fluorescent safety vest. 'My plane ticket gets me a tarmac tour guide with a snazzy jacket.'

'So I see. Oh, there's my case.' Grateful for the distraction, I step forward to snatch the khaki duffle bag from the cart and bump into fluoro-safety guy. When I turn back, Zac is still sitting there. *Of course he is!*

'The company's sending a car,' he explains. 'It's running late, but if you need a lift somewhere …'

'You know what, Zac?' We both move away from the milling crowd. 'You're right. I was going to the school reunion for the wrong reason. Such events are perfect for the pretty and popular girls to monopolise conversations, show off husbands and play pass-the-picture games by gushing over photos of their equally attractive offspring. The event hasn't even begun and I'm already questioning my worth and my achievements. Best I go home.'

Zac looks at the departures board. 'Seriously? And face another plane trip so soon? I'd better track down a Gin and Tonic for you. Please?'

I nod and suggest a coffee. 'First, let me change my ticket.'

Laughing easily over our lattes, any earlier concerns gone, I wonder what's happened to my usual clumsy, nerve-charged conversation.

'Can I ask you something, Zac?' My curiosity and courage are aroused by an urgency to learn more about this man before, again, saying goodbye. 'What happened?'

He flashes a cheeky grin. 'Geez, if only I had a dollar ...'

I'm immediately mortified. 'Sorry. Asking is *so* incredibly rude.'

'No, it's not. Staring is rude. Asking is fine,' he reassures. 'Telling my story is how I make a living. So, get comfortable, Amazing Grayce, and I'll give you the free version.' He makes a point of settling back into his wheelchair and pausing. 'I understood the risks.' He begins. 'It was my ninety-ninth jump. My skydiving buddy had an equipment problem. The only way to help was to try slowing him down midair. I had to decide how quickly.' The memory eclipses the usual sparkle in his eyes. 'Despite the danger to myself, I reached him and I didn't let go. If I hadn't got him down, his wife would've killed me!' he adds with a grin.

'You saved him?'

'The trees did. They broke both our falls, only I ended up in this thing.'

We sit without speaking for the first time since meeting. It's an easy silence, broken only by the jarring volume of the airport speakers.

'Final boarding call for Flight QF555.'

'That must be yours and my driver awaits.' He skulls the cold coffee dregs. 'I should let you go.'

Please don't, Zac, I want to say. *Don't let me go.*

This is my moment of truth, the risk clear and I can feel myself falling. Time to make a decision—quickly.

'You okay, Grayce?'

'No.' Standing tall with my arms folded across my chest, I feign confidence. 'I need to ask you something.' I swallow. It's not easy with a lump of trepidation in my throat. 'Are you still a good catch, Zac?'

His face crumples into a smile and he eyes me as if I have the words *strange girl* scribbled on my forehead. 'Why do you ask?'

'Because I'm not ready to board a plane home. I don't think I'll be making the most of my life if I leave Sunflower today.'

'Where *do* you want to go?'

'After meeting you I have no idea about anything, other than I'm ready to take a chance. I want to jump and I'm kind of hoping you're still a good catch.'

Zac whoops and pulls me back down into the seat opposite him. He leans forward and takes both my hands, pressing them to his knees.

'I'm a great catch, whichever way you want to interpret that, Amazing Grayce. But,' he says, his squint serious, 'you need to do something first. It's a kind of ritual I suggest to my audiences when I'm suggesting they take a leap of faith and there's a word the brave yell.'

'Let me guess.' I gaze into the azure abyss of his eyes and prepare to jump. 'Geronimo!'

THE MALE RUN

'You'll love this, Ellie,' Jane says. 'It's what you need,' Jane says. 'Believe me,' she says.

But I'm unconvinced. The last thing my sister thought I needed had been two days in a Tibetan-inspired retreat in the hills around Toowoomba. Besides, how can my sister know what I need, when I don't?

Still wiping sleep from my eyes, surprised by the sun's warmth this early in the day, I make a mental list of things that might fall under Jane's heading of *What Ellie Needs*. My mind comes up with the usual: a lottery win, world peace, and to discover a cure for heart disease so I'm out of a job. None of these, however, require a pre-dawn departure from the very comfortable Sunflower Motor Inn only to wait on a dusty airstrip.

'Let me guess, Jane. You've chartered a private jet and we're off to a tropical paradise.'

'As if!' she scoffs.

'Then tell me why you've dragged me back here on Friday morning, having only flown in yesterday, or I'm going back to the motel.'

'Geez, Ellie, you've always been a spoilsport.' Jane's words, spoken like a true younger sister, take Ellie back twenty years. 'Okay, okay,'

Jane grumbles. 'If you insist I spoil the surprise. You're here for the mail run.'

I raise an interrogative eyebrow. '*Male* run? I don't understand. Why?'

'Because I thought it would be a fun thing for you to do, Ellie. Remember that word—fun?'

The sound of scraping metal startles us both and a stocky silhouette emerges from the shadows of the airport's single hangar.

'Whoa! Hottie at twelve o'clock.' Jane's whisper of appreciation barely moves her lips as her hands complete a quick and flirty fix of her hair.

While my sister requires little help to look spectacular, I am cognisant my early-morning appearance is less striking and I could have made more effort with my mousey brown waves, especially given the hottie heading our way. Mid-to-late forties, clean-shaven, wearing dark navy shorts and a khaki short-sleeve shirt with epaulettes on broad shoulders, the man sets the Tom—*Top Gun*—Cruise sunglasses on the brim of his peak cap and smiles.

'Good morning, ladies.'

'Well, hello!' Jane dangles a damsel's hand in his direction. 'You must be Jack?'

'I am. And I assume one of you is Eleanor, my companion for this little adventure.'

'That's me. I'm Eleanor. And I'm sorry.' My stare shuts Jane down. 'I'm sorry to say, if this male run—whatever it involves—requires me getting on another aeroplane, then I'm afraid my prankster sister has outdone herself. I'm not a fan of small planes. Yesterday's flight was bad enough. Terra firma is my friend.' Like a desperate Dorothy wishing herself home, I click my heels three times, but all the action does is raise a tiny dust storm to coat my brown canvas pumps beige. 'As intriguing as a *male* run sounds—and I won't ask—I'm seeking neither companion, exercise, nor adventure today.'

'Right then,' the hottie says. 'You've made that crystal clear, much like the sky today. Personally, I can't wait to get up there.'

'I, on the other hand, need to recover from yesterday's flight from hell,' I tell the man.

'Too much air turbulence?' he enquires.

Jane is quick to answer. 'Too much in-flight celebrity for Ellie. The guys from that new *Let's Get High* television show were sitting two seats in front of us. They amused everyone.'

'In all the wrong ways,' I add, pleased with the man's reciprocal smirk.

My sister squares her shoulders, ready to defend her love of reality TV—probably by repeating her insistence that there's therapeutic value in laughing at others. Only two nights ago, she'd suggested I apply for the next season of *The Bachelorette* because, in her words, 'a surgical theatre is not conducive to hooking up with a bloke'.

'What are the odds of them being on the plane?' Jane says. 'I wonder what brings them to Sunflower? Guess we'll have to wait and see, eh?'

I'm not sure which is more vexing. A swarm of sticky flies buzzing around my head, or my sister's words buzzing my brain and pricking every probability bubble except one.

'Oh, Jane, please tell me you haven't signed on for something to do with that show. Are they filming us now? Are they here somewhere and about to jump out from behind a building?' My gaze takes in the airstrip, darting between the nearby hangars, and the larger terminal on the commercial tarmac in the distance. 'A ruse to involve me in some sort of mile-high, speed dating show—'

'Ellie, no, I would never—'

Far too annoyed to look at my sister, I flash a hand in her direction and focus on the man in the costume.

'It's Jack, isn't it?' I ask. 'Look, I'm so sorry for the confusion.' A flash of my palm in Jane's direction demands her silence. 'Don't take my displeasure personally. Whatever *The Male Run* dating rules are, as a contestant you have the looks to make it through to the end—whatever that may be—and while I won't be taking part, no matter what my sister thinks, I promise to watch out for you when the show airs. Oh, and if phone voting is required, you can count on me. You're not only a great sport, Jack, I enjoy a happy ever after as much as anyone, and I wish you and your potential dates well.'

'Ellie, this is a mistake.'

'You're right, Jane.' On this occasion I agree with my sister. Being openly condescending is never appropriate. 'But I'm handling the situation.'

'If I can get a word in, ladies,' Jack interjects. 'There's obviously been a huge mix-up and I wish I could offer you a refund, but the company booking policy is not my rule. I'll leave you both to work things out, but before I do,' Jack checks his watch, 'let me assure you, Eleanor, I'm unaware of any reality shows and I'm not into speed dating, on or off the screen. The only passengers I want on the plane over there are the paying kind—and pronto—because my reality is pretty much scheduled for me.' He points to one of two small aircraft. 'I take my job seriously and while we'll make a cruising altitude of around twenty-seven thousand-feet, I'm usually too preoccupied being a real pilot and adhering to my contracted postal deliveries to take part in a mile-high club with a passenger. As lovely as the idea sounds, the only thing on offer today is a mail delivery tour to outlying stations, as arranged with your sister.'

My tongue, lolling about in my mouth, makes speaking a challenge. 'I, ah, you mean … You deliver the M–A–I–L?' I swallow the next smart remark, my expression pleading. 'Jane? Why?'

'Ellie, honey, I dragged you to Sunflower this week as company because I didn't want you to be alone on your birthday. Or did you think I'd forget?'

'I was hoping so, yes,' I tell her.

'Well, I didn't and while I'm slaving away in a training room, teaching old miners new safety tricks, you'll be on an adventure. On Saturday I plan on showing you around town.'

My head hurts with the words I'm unable to speak aloud: *I don't need an adventure, Jane. I need my life in Sydney, wrapped up in my cosy cocoon of self-pity where I've been happily miserable for months.*

'Listen, ladies,' the pilot says. 'Email me your bank details and I'll see what I can do. But to be honest, Eleanor, like your sister, I also enjoy company on my trips. So, if you do have a change of heart and wish to join me, there's time. I still have my pre-flight checks to do. If not, it's been, ah, interesting. Thanks!'

'Come on, Ellie,' Jane pleads as the pilot walks away. 'What have you got to lose? Go, and for a day forget everything. Have fun.'

I remain totally flabbergasted and shake my head. 'Why here and now?'

'Okay, the truth is, Ellie, I heard the mail run provides a bird's-eye view of the entire Ruby Garnet mine. At the very least, I thought you'd be interested in seeing where I work from a different angle. After all, haven't I grown up with you telling me to see things from your perspective?'

Did I say that? I want to ask her. I refrain. 'Jane, I don't mean to appear ungrateful. Yes, I'm interested in your job, and I am curious about the tour but—'

'No buts.' My sister waggles a finger, a trait she's picked up from me. 'You're going.' Jane hoists the small backpack over my shoulder and frees the shirt collar that catches underneath.

Today, my little sister is the one to fuss; to nudge me, like I'd mothered her on the first day of school over two decades ago. All the years I've wondered what sort of woman she would grow up to be and here she is—a highly respected safety consultant taking charge and worrying about me for a change.

'Ellie, you raised me to ask questions, to be strong, and to break down barriers and I have, while you've spent too much time in sterilised operating theatres, staring at minuscule portions of patients through a microscope. Go flying, Sis. Go … appreciate the big open spaces, enjoy country air for a change. Breathe.'

Once we're settled into the cramped cockpit, Jack fits my headset, then his own. With any luck, there'll be minimal conversation. Until recently, most of my exchanges have involved speaking in medical terms with my surgical team. So small talk with strangers is more awkward than it need be. As he's adjusting the microphone, his hand close to my nose, I detect something. *Grease?* While not an unpleasant or bad smell, it's a change from the sterile scent of a surgical theatre. As for my ordinarily steady hands—for which my patients are grateful —a slick of sweat makes tightening the seatbelt tricky.

'A few deep breaths,' Jack says with a smile, his voice loud and clear in both ears. 'You'll be fine, Eleanor, but should you require a sick bag, you'll find one there.'

'Call me Ellie, Ellie Porter, and I don't get airsick.' Immediately sorry for the snappish retort, I am grateful when he grins.

'I hear you, loud and clear, Ellie Porter,' he says after adjusting his own mouthpiece. 'If you have questions, ask me before I start the in-flight safety procedure.'

'There is one thing I should check.' I try sounding upbeat. 'Does this machine of yours have an eject button for boorish passengers with excess baggage?'

Jack peers over his sunglasses and tugs the navy peak cap over blond locks—the sort that are used to getting their own way. 'Haven't needed any such switch—yet, Ellie, and you're hardly boorish.' The plane's engine kicks over and Jack's volume rises with it. 'You have a sense of humour and you don't throw up on planes. All positives from where I sit.'

'You sound like a glass-half-full kind of guy.'

He stops what he's doing and looks back from the myriad dials and switches. 'I am these days. The only baggage allowed on my plane is the mail. Any other stuff stays behind for you to collect once we land. Deal?' His smile remains small, but the tan lines etched at the corners of his mouth and eyes suggest Jack has laughed a lot in his lifetime.

I used to laugh once and I might have managed a semblance of a glass-half-full person, were I not so nervous about the aircraft gathering speed.

'Your adventure begins, Ellie Porter,' Jack announces while looking at everything but me.

I like him. I admire his unguarded gusto and that he sees only positives, when my baggage could ground a jumbo jet.

'So, how does this mail run work?'

Jack launches into his spiel about the plane, the service's history, and how he and his once-a-week schedule remain the only regular contact for many isolated landowners. The world he describes is so removed from mine. He flies hundreds of kilometres several times a week, whereas collecting my daily mail requires twenty paces from the door of my inner-city terrace to the tiny tin box on the front fence.

When the aircraft finally levels out, so do I, surprisingly.

'So, Mr Postman, how far does a mail run take you?'

'This one's an eight hundred-kilometre round trip,' he replies.

'And what exactly do you deliver?'

'A variety of things, including food and medicines to cattle stations, Aboriginal missions and outposts. Mostly I deliver the supplies you city types find down the street in an air-conditioned shopping centre.'

'Hmm, yes, us pampered city folk! We're a lazy lot. And spoilt rotten.' I clip my sentences to make my point. 'Damn air-conditioned dens of debauched consumerism! Perfect for us city types to grab a double-mocha-latte-grande-on-soy.'

'I apologise,' he says. 'Stereotyping is not an attractive trait. Some-times my humour misses the mark. One of my bad habits.' A danger-ously beguiling sideways smile totally exonerates him. 'So, did your sister drag you out here kicking and screaming?'

'Not quite,' I say. 'I admit the name Sunflower made me curious and Jane thinks I need to get out more and embrace life; although how life-changing can a mail run be?'

'You changed *my* very average day by being here,' he says. 'I'm always grateful for company.'

I stare out the side window at a patchwork of shapes that stain the landscape so spectacularly the vista surely calls for more than a lazy cliché. *Patchwork* might suit, but that reminds me of cosy quilts—soft and malleable, and something made with love. What I'm seeing is a sunbaked blanket with the crisscrossing seams of sparse shrubbery and dried-up waterways desperate for rain. Nothing comforting about that.

Jack's voice penetrates the headset. 'A country not for the faint-hearted,' he says. 'The outback reminds me of a delinquent child; one that pushes the boundaries—requiring discipline and demanding love, while giving little in return.'

Jack's analogy might have been describing Ellie's early relationship with her sister. Poor, darling Jane had been too young to understand the significance of two coffins in the church that day, but from the moment she did, her hurt quickly turned to anger and a need to break every rule. The school system gave up on Jane. Ellie never did.

'Stay sharp,' Jack says. 'Any minute you'll see the latest Ruby Garnet excavation and processing area out your window. On our return we'll buzz the headquarters. Jane requested it when she booked. Said she'd be between training sessions and looking out for us.'

My baby sister, I muse. All grown up, and a professional trainer. She had to work so hard. Knowing her expertise is integral and she stands tall and confident at the front of a classroom, teaching work-place risk minimisation strategies to workers, makes me forget and forgive every teenage transgression.

'What's that in the distance?' I point to a long brown line of something snaking its way over the vast plain below us.

'Our first stop,' Jack says. 'No-Go Creek Station. What you're seeing is about five hundred of the twenty thousand head of cattle being herded into a satellite yard.'

As the plane pitches, and the high wing design of the Cessna provides uninterrupted views of the rich, red canvas below I ask, 'Have you always lived here, Jack?'

'Nope,' he replied. 'Sydney-based with a commercial airline, but those pilots tend to spend more time in the air than on the ground. I needed balance. I wanted greater control over my life, and a place to call home. I found Sunflower, where I could split my working week between the mail run and the Royal Flying Doctor Service. That's when I'm not starring in reality TV dating programs and partaking in mile-high shenanigans with my passengers.'

Laughing feels good. I like Jack's guffaw and his grin which is still in place when we touch down, the landing smooth despite a runway shortened by a startled mob of emus.

'You can let go now.' He eyes my white-knuckled grip. 'Time to stretch those legs and deliver the mail.' He reaches into the back seat and drags a weatherproof canvas satchel onto my lap.

'To where? There's nothing but trees and a worn track.'

'Leave the mail bag this side of that black stump,' he says.

I scoff. 'Another city girl joke? All part of the adventure? A ritualistic initiation for the unwary? A tourist photo opportunity, perhaps?'

He doesn't smile. 'No, seriously, there's a bucket at the burnt out tree trunk. The empty feedbag stays over the top to keep the rain out. You can help me, if you like. You'll find a brick to keep the cover in place until the parcels are all collected. Stay on the plane if you prefer,' he adds when I don't move, 'but most people like the interactive aspect of the mail run.'

'Then I suppose I'll do my bit.'

After climbing down from the cockpit, wishing I'd worn trousers, I tread the twenty-or-so paces to the drop-off point and peer inside the bucket and the blackened tree stump.

'Is this legal?' I call to Jack. 'Aren't there mail-handling laws?'

A deep belly laugh reaches me and he hollers a reply. 'Come on, city girl, jump in and let's go.'

Back at the plane, I hoist myself into the passenger seat like a pro: no awkward tangle of limbs, less self-consciousness, and with fewer reservations about the next leg of my mail run adventure. 'Where to now, Captain Jack?'

'Jumbuluk is thirty minutes away. Settle in for the spiel,' he says.

◡

There must be three dozen people, in, on, or leaning against two rusty station wagons and a small tray-top truck at the end of the skinny runway. Among them, two boys with identical smiles and wide brown eyes are jumping up and down on the spot.

'And here we are,' Jack announces while bringing the Cessna to a standstill and reaching into the back seat.

The boys clap hands when Jack jumps from the plane donning a purple party hat. They squeal louder when out of his breast pocket comes a paper whistle which he uses as a pitch pipe before launching into a solo chorus of 'Happy Birthday'. The excited pair snatch the lolly bags he brings out from behind his back and run off, with a dozen children in pursuit. After Jack introduces Ellie to the elders, the adults take charge of the six delivered cartons, cramming them—and everyone else—into the dust-coated vehicles. The cars disappear in a plume of red powder and we reboard the plane, our conversation shifting to something more personal.

'I understand Jane is based at the mine's headquarters in the city, Ellie, but what do you do back in the big smoke?'

I edit my answer. 'Surgeon.' Or should I have said ex-surgeon, given I walked away from my position three months ago?

'Wow,' he says, 'I didn't expect—'

I interrupt to finish the sentence for him. 'A latte-swilling surgeon aboard your plane?'

'To be honest, I rarely get professional people on my mail run—mostly retired grey nomads because they see me and Jelly as the poor man's Bill Peach Air Cruise.'

'You've named your plane Jelly? As in "I like Aeroplane Jelly"?' Ellie refrained from singing the old advertising jingle.

'Yep, although not everyone gets the connection. The nomads do but, like I said, having someone more my age is a change. Jelly's a beauty, isn't she?' His hand strokes the door moulding. 'She's a capable, rugged, load-carrying Cessna Caravan. I prefer my girls comfortable, dependable, and with grunt.'

'That's good to know,' I tell him.

'Sure is. She has a climb rate of three-hundred-and-seventy-six feet per minute, has a maximum cruising speed of around one-hundred-and-eighty knots and, while she can cruise comfortably at twenty-five-thousand feet, we'll be staying down around nine. You see?' he says, sounding chuffed. 'A good pilot knows everything about their partner. Although not my first, this old girl and I have been together so long I recognise every beat of her heart.'

The self-conscious clearing of his throat and a slight pink blush to his neck is endearing. 'Jelly is very comfortable and fully equipped, even down to the snazzy first-aid box I installed.' His hand brushes my knee as he indicates the red bag strapped to the floor near my foot. 'Out here it helps to be ready for anything and to expect the unexpected. Open 'er up, Doc. Check it out.'

My first thought is the supplies are indeed extensive and impressive. My second is the contents are rather deficient should we drop out of the sky from nine thousand feet.

And so, deliberately leaving the thought behind, I scan the vista ahead. 'So, where next, Captain Jack?'

He points to serpentine curves of green; a striking contrast to the seemingly endless carpet of red we've been flying over. 'Kilby River Station. Prepare for landing, city girl.'

'Roger that!' I giggle—yes, I giggle—and tug my seatbelt tight.

On the edge of the runway sits a ute with two mangy brown kelpies sprawled and panting in the back.

The man smoking a pipe and leaning against the door calls out to us. 'Helper today, Jack?'

'Don, this is Ellie from the city.' Jack tosses a sack into the ute and ruffles the ears on both dogs.

'G'day!' Don extends his arm as I approach and I feel the hardened callouses and grit of a hard-working hand. 'The missus'll be disappointed she's not here today. She don't see many of 'er kind out here much.' His face is a series of wrinkles and all seem to radiate from the corner of two squinty eyes. 'Dragged her away from her flash life decades ago and plonked her in Kilby River. She thanks me every bleedin' day, too.' His grin exposes two chipped teeth; the accompanying wink shows a wicked sense of humour. 'Hop in and we'll get out of this sun.'

'Hop in?' I question.

'Too hot to walk. Get in there,' he shouts as a third dog appears from under the vehicle.'

I hesitate and hold Jack back with a sharp yank on his shirtsleeve. I'm about to ask if I should leave breadcrumbs when he grins and, holding the ute passenger door open, says in a low voice, 'Sometimes I deliver more than the mail. Out here, a bit of face-to-face chatter is better than any letter. Don't worry, though, it's not a long drive and it's factored into the schedule'.

Don pulls the ute to a stop outside a sizeable homestead with a typical wraparound veranda on all sides and a high-pitched tin roof. Four screaming children come running from every direction, while a fifth —a teenage girl—stands demurely at the veranda steps.

'Afraid the tea and cake might not be to the usual standard,' Don says as he parks the ute. 'Bethy, me eldest girl, did 'er best, but she's not 'er mother. Come in and make yourselves at home.'

When we stop to remove our shoes, adding them to the long line of upturned boots and a scattering of rubber thongs, Jack explains— again in a low voice—about Don's wife. 'Surgery first, a donated organ, and constant follow-ups; all done thousands of kilometres away and without her family. Such is the challenge of regionally based organ recipients. You must understand how it is,' Jack says.

Did she? Could Dr Eleanor Porter, city born and educated, her pathway paved with opportunity, relate to the hardship and isolation of life on the land? Even after losing both parents, there'd been support people and organisations a phone call away. The homestead in which she's standing is hundreds of kilometres from anywhere. The place is a little hectic and missing a mother's touch, but the aroma of something freshly baked fills the air. The two children chase each other around the sofas, while the three youngest have the mail sack at the centre of the floor rug. With the usual dolls, toy horses, and Lego pieces pushed aside, the boys let envelopes and small parcels tumble from the sack and onto the floor.

'Hey, you lot, take it easy,' Don warns. 'Pick every one of 'em back up and put 'em on the table.'

'But, Dad, there's no rain,' one child whines. 'Mum said she'd send rain.'

'Maybe next time, matey. I'm sure Mum's tryin' her best. She's probably busy.'

'Where's the treats?' another asks. 'Mum always sends treats.'

'How about this package?' Jack produces the parcel from behind his back. 'Silly me almost forgot. At least I think it's yours. Let me see.' Jack holds the parcel high, feigning short-sightedness. 'It's addressed: "To My Beautiful Children". Is that you lot?' There's a squabble to take control of the package before the day's surprises spill over the floor: fruity roll-ups for the twins, Pez dispensers for the older boys, and what looks like a flavoured lip gloss for Bethy.

After tea and cake on the veranda, Jack helps Don load the ute with return parcels and Bethy, now with shiny lips, is inside playing mother to one twin. As I join her in the living room, the other twin scrambles over my lap, fascinated by my sparkly earrings.

I notice Bethy fall quiet and assume her mother's note, folded on her lap, is causing the melancholy.

'The cake was lovely,' I say. 'Is your mum as good a cook as you?'

No response.

'Bethy?' Concern stiffens my tone as the girl's face turns puffy and red, obvious enough to scoot the child from my lap and stand. 'Bethy, what's wrong?'

I drop to my knees in front of her to check the girl's pulse: weak, heart racing, obvious respiratory distress. *Anaphylaxis? How?* The subdued Bethy has not eaten since their arrival—not even her own cake. *Think, Ellie, think.*

I force myself to stand back, to breathe, and to see the girl; not the patient, or an anaesthetised part of one. A minute ago, she'd been putting on makeup and—*Makeup!* Could the reaction be from lip gloss? I grab the strawberry-coloured tube from her lap and scan the small print for allergen warnings. *Nothing.*

Voices register in my ears. The men are returning to the veranda.

'Jack! Don!' I scream over the twins crying in stereo. 'It's Bethy. Something's wrong. Help me get her to the floor.'

Before the screen door has time to bang, a worried father is crouching by his daughter's side. 'What's happened?'

'Does Bethy suffer from anaphylaxis, Don?'

'No, no.' He grips her shoulders where she lies glassy-eyed. 'Bethy! Bethy, sweetie!'

'Let me help, Ellie.' Jack's calmness is reassuring. 'Tell me what I can do and it's done.'

'The plane. The first-aid box. The Epi-pen. And Jack … ' I hear the warning in my voice as I check the clock on the wall. 'Hurry.'

When Jack returns, I administer the shot of adrenaline into Bethy's thigh and comfort her while Don reassures and soothes the rest of his panic-stricken brood.

'Losing 'er would break my heart, Ellie.' The shimmering veil of early tears is a heartbreaking contrast to the work-weary face. 'You docs 'ave got a little magic in ya for sure. Imagine if you hadn't come along with Jack today.'

'I'm glad I came, too.'

'Me three.' Jack adds with a grin. 'And I reckon another brew is in order. I'll put the kettle on.'

'Bethy will be fine,' I reassure Don after Jack leaves. 'But to avoid future scares I suggest a trip to the city and a thorough allergy screen.'

There's a tugging on my shirt tail. 'You fixed my sister,' says a small voice. The boy's eyes are red, his cheeks ruddy and wet from tears. 'Can you do magic on my mum now?'

I drop to my haunches to engage the boy's attention. 'Your mum already has people waving magic wands all around her, but I can do something special, just for you, if you want.' The boy's head bobs. 'When Jack's plane is so high that I can see all the way to the hospital, I'll be able to blow her a big kiss from all of you. Okay?'

'Hold that thought,' Jack announces from the doorway. 'Jelly's grounded.'

'Grounded? Why? What's wrong?'

'Heard some chatter on Don's radio just now about a dust storm brewing. The storm will probably miss Kilby River Station, but with Sunflower bearing the brunt we can't risk flying in.' He must see worry in my eyes because he adds, 'Ellie, I asked Base to advise your sister we're safe and staying put. Sorry, mate.' Jack winks at Don. 'You've got company overnight.'

'Bloody hell!' Don lets out a small yelp of delight. 'You won't get a complaint out of me. Lucky I got a whole beast butchered. You must be on cooking detail, Jack, lad. I'll fix the sleeping arrangements.' Don is already heading out of the room when he calls back, 'Bethy will bunk with me so I can keep an eye on 'er, and the twins can share her bed, so you and Ellie can have the twin beds, unless of course ....'

'Err, twin beds are fine, Don,' Jack says aloud before casting a silent *sorry* and coy shrug.

U

The sun hasn't yet set when Don settles his exhausted children for the night and I check on Bethy. When I return, the two men are in deck chairs on the front porch, a discussion about climate change in full swing and getting louder until they find common ground mocking ignorant politicians. Only when the conversation turns to sports do I join in. Soon after, Don bids us both goodnight.

For a while Jack and I revisit our lunchtime conversation; a friendly word war about inequality in various sports. When he concedes defeat and our laughter fades, we share a comfortable silence until I stifle a yawn.

'A bigger adventure than planned,' Jack states.

'And exhausting.'

'Doing something different tuckers me out in good ways,' he says. 'Not sure how surgeons stand in one place for hours. When I quit full-time flying, I took a flight manager's job but found sitting behind a desk too long made Jack a very cranky bloke.'

'I can't imagine Jack cranky,' I say.

'Sunflower has taught me a lot about myself. I learned to smile again, largely because small-town locals smile and say g'day and, well, we live in a town named Sunflower. How can you not smile?'

I ponder the notion. 'In my profession, no one would know if I was smiling or not. Surgical masks make it impossible to tell.'

'They'd know,' Jack says without hesitation. 'Your eyes do this thing.' He leans close and I want him to kiss me. Instead, he cups a palm over my mouth and my nose and says, 'Go on. Smile.'

I do as asked, surprised to discover a genuine one is not difficult at all. Having a gorgeous man so close helps.

'As I thought,' he says. 'Your eyes have it. People see your smile. By the way, did I wish you a happy birthday yet?' He pulls me by the hand to kiss me on the cheek. 'Happy birthday, Dr Ellie Porter. Hope you've enjoyed your day.'

'I've had no negative thoughts about my job. That's unusual.'

'Hard to turn off when you're dedicated, I guess, and you clearly are—and good at what you do, too.'

My smile fades. 'I'm good at what I do because the procedure is precise and repeated over and over. At the same time, however, we do have to be ready for those moments when things don't go to plan.'

'Piloting a plane is also about procedure and preparation,' Jack says.

'Ah, yes,' I respond, 'but you're in control before you sit in the seat and start her up. You're familiar with Jelly inside and out; you know what she does and when. She doesn't lie to you about the food she's had, or the few too many drinks she consumed instead of fasting the night before surgery. And she doesn't keep the information about the party drugs she thought didn't count as *nil by mouth*.'

The same anxiety grips my chest as I flash back to that point in time when I'd figured it out—but too late. 'And because she doesn't tell you, Jack, you're not expecting complications like her stomach regurgitating to fill her lungs. You don't expect to lose her during a routine procedure and spend every second of every day questioning what you did and didn't do trying to save her. And you didn't have to tell her parents how you—' My hands scrub the wetness from my face and a groan. 'Good grief! What a mess I am. I haven't spoken about that to anyone other than Jane.'

'You are a very lovely mess,' Jack says, 'and it can help to talk. Lucky for you, I'm a superb listener.'

Without hesitating, chairs rocking in unison under a giant moon, I tell him everything.

U

'Thank you, Jack. Today has helped more than you know. Working through Bethy's symptoms reminded me why I wanted to do medicine in the first place; yet here I am a decade later with patients brought into surgery already diagnosed and prepped by others because surgical efficiency is what keeps the theatre administrators happy.'

Passion pumps my heart rate up a notch. I used to get a kick out of the rush, I used to love my work, and today reminded me why I wanted to be a doctor. 'Don't get me wrong,' I tell Jack. 'My surgical team and I know our job and we do it by rote, one patient after the other. Today, however, Bethy's condition gave my brain a much-needed workout. I observed, diagnosed, treated and, thanks to the dust storm, I'll be here in the morning to follow up. I'm certain she'll be fine, but that's not always the case in my experience. Not everyone gets a good result.'

Jack's silence says he knows, and the tightening of his hand around mine tells me he cares. We stay sitting that way until the night air grows too chilly and Jack stands.

'I guess we should hit the hay, city girl. Thanks to the dust storm, I get to spend the night with you. Admittedly, it's in twin beds,' he grins, shrugs, 'but a bloke can dream.'

I stand, I lean into him, and we embrace until I pull away, smiling back with a challenge. 'Last one to the bathroom is a rotten egg.'

◡

'Ellie, Ellie, wake up, quickly.'

'Jack?' I wake to the pink glow of first light tinging the picture window. 'Are we leaving already?'

'Yes, get dressed.'

As neither of us undressed before falling into our twin beds, there is no *getting dressed* required, but I'm slow to register the urgency in Jack's whispered words. Something about an accident, a quad bike and a crushed stockman.

He has my attention.

'The local fire brigade crew is on site,' he says, 'but before moving the patient they'll need a proper medical assessment. The closest person is over an hour away by car. They've called the Royal Flying Docs, but the Sunflower landing strip got a hammering last night and the aircraft needs a safety check. That's where you and I come in,' he explains. 'Jelly can put us at the scene in fifteen minutes—max. I told them I have a doctor aboard.'

'Of course,' Ellie's already up. 'What are we waiting for?'

◡

There's less laughter during this morning's flight. In fact, we barely utter a word as Jelly streaks across a clear sky showing no sign of the dreaded dust storm, or of the devastating scene awaiting us. After a rough landing—and Jack's million apologies—we're being driven in a car that rattles and shudders over a pockmarked plain of brown shrubs. On my lap is Jack's basic first-aid kit. Could be worse, I remind myself, trying the glass-half-full approach.

The driver—a woman in her seventies—meets the plane and says little, except to update us on how far we still have to drive.

'What do you know about the patient, Sonya?' I ask.

When she tells me he's her husband, I am blown away by her composure, and I tell her as much. Her reply further shows a stoicism I rarely witness.

'Just the way we are out here, love,' she says, voice flat. 'Thank God for people like you and the other docs. We'd be a lot less lucky without your help. I'll park here. He's down there, in the ditch.'

My heart thuds as I rush from the car, almost tripping as adrenaline surges through my body and makes me question my capability. Thank goodness Jack's close enough to grab my arm and save my fall. Hospital corridors rarely require a full run, and rabbit holes, ruts and cow manure are not my usual obstacles.

Thankfully, it's early and the outback heat is yet to turn the ground under the patient iron hot. We negotiate the broken paddock fence, now a tangle of wire and quad bike, to reach the rider who has serious ligature marks on his neck.

Lucky man, I say to myself. Had he damaged a major blood vessel and caused a vertebral artery dissection, death from subarachnoid haemorrhage would have been certain and immediate. But, while the wire's force is clearly severe, and it has stopped short of penetrating the skin, there's more going on. I need to figure out what.

A breathing patient is a positive start, but after a vehicle rollover, especially a quad bike, I can't discount abdominal or pelvic injury. Also, crushing of the chest wall can cause asphyxiation and death. Sonya had said the man, though semi-conscious now, remained alert long enough to make contact by SAT phone. Another promising sign, I tell myself. I listen to his heart and lungs the best I can, aware an ultrasound is the only way to confirm a pneumothorax. If one of his lungs collapses, I can adapt the instruments I've got to pierce his chest and release the pressure.

I know I'm capable of trying whatever is needed to save a life, but I pray I won't need any invasive procedure, especially with a loved one looking on. I also hope more help is on its way.

At that very moment, as the man—his name is Graham—stops breathing and I begin chest compressions, the *whop-whop-whop* of helicopter blades drowns out Sonya's mumbled prayer. Our help sets down in an adjacent paddock. Any minute there'll be a neck brace available, a backboard, a defibrillator and drugs, but for now I stay focused and will my patient to live. I see nothing other than a husband, father and beloved granddad, and hear nothing but my counting until Jack's hands tug me from behind. At first, I fight back with a flick of my shoulders. Then I hear his words.

'Stop, Ellie. You can stop. They have a pulse. It's strong. You saved him.'

◡

With Sonya and Graham airborne and en route to the hospital, Jack and I drive to the neighbouring property. Mal will take care of Kilby River Station until Graham is back on deck, and he'll drop us back to Jelly, but not until he's thanked us with a hearty country breakfast of eggs and bacon. It's a country thing, I'm told.

When we do say goodbye to Mal, I suspect we'll be friends forever.

◡

My emotions refuse to stay in check on the flight back to Sunflower and the feeling is new. Since I was eighteen years of age, after my Dad's heart gave out and he drove the car and Mum off a bridge and into a river, I've had to be strong for Jane. I learned to hide my emotions and lead with my head rather than my heart. There was no trusting a broken heart. Years later, as a specialist surgeon inserting stents to save lives, I know every microscopic detail of my patient's heart and how to fix it.

I'm thinking what a shame I can't mend my own when I feel it— my heart—banging inside my body: energised and strong and fervent. Forty-eight hours ago I was dreading this mail run. *And now?*

'Talk to me, Ellie.' Jack's voice penetrates my headphones. 'What's going on inside that clever head of yours?'

'Here's me thinking Jane couldn't top last year's birthday present. Don't ask,' I warn before Jack has a chance.

'Has she?' he asks. 'The mail run was an okay present after all?'

'More than okay,' I reply. 'This adventure has made me realise what's missing in my life.'

'Ah, adventure maybe?' he quips.

'No!' I gently whack his shoulder and giggle. It's a sound I'm getting used to hearing again. 'I'm referring to the simple things: genuine friendship, the taste of farm-fresh eggs and home-smoked bacon, feeling four seasons in one day and the joy of reading the mail.'

Jack laughs. 'As in M–A–I–L?'

'As in L–E–T–T–E–R–S,' I explain. 'No one sends actual letters anymore. In their place, we get faceless emails and nameless text messages in hurriedly written shorthand with smiley faces to soften the words. Life out here seems slower, easier.'

'Not always,' Jack says. 'People presume country folk enjoy simple lives when the reality is, we face challenges every day, but we avoid complicating matters with all that city stuff.'

'Maybe I should give the city away for a while. I could buy chickens, take a holiday, write a postcard or a letter. I miss folding the note to make it fit before buying the stamp, licking the seal and writing the address.' I lean my head back and close my eyes, the hum of the aircraft soothing. 'My life is an envelope, Jack. Blank and empty, no purpose, and no destination.'

'Sounds like you're set to collect that baggage you left behind yesterday morning.'

A click in my headset and the Air Controller's voice lets me avoid answering.

'Could be wet weather on the way,' Jack says as we dip and soar towards an early full moon shrouded in cloud. 'Hopefully enough to wash away the layer of dust, but not ruin your night, assuming you and your sister have plans.'

I huff a laugh. 'Thankfully, the birthday is over, so unless Jane has another surprise in store I have nothing planned but plenty to contemplate.'

The plane's wheels touching down bring both relief and regret.

The mail run is done.

I find Jane waiting; her face is a teary mess.

'Oh my God, Ellie, I've been so worried.'

'I was in good hands, Jane. Come on, let's get inside the terminal and out of the rain.'

After calming my sister, I leave her with a cafe latte from the vending machine and I excuse myself to find Jack; he's in a hangar inspecting Jelly's undercarriage.

'I wanted to tell you again, you and your mail run, while not what I was expecting, sure made my birthday memorable. Everything was great. Really great.'

'Yes, you were,' Jack responds, 'And I'm glad. Pass me that rag, would you?'

'Oh, sure.' I pick up the ratty T-shirt and thrust it into his outstretched hand.

'By the way, Ellie,' he grunted as a hand slipped and a spanner clanged onto the concrete floor. 'I checked. Our Royal Flying Doctor Service loves latte-swilling surgeons. Apparently, we really like the ones who laugh, don't get airsick, and save lives. So, if you want to send a job application, I can write the address on a blank envelope.'

I laugh freely and loudly, and it feels good. 'I'll give it serious thought, but right now my brain needs food before I can consider any decisions. So, Captain Jack, unless you're too busy with your best girl—'

'Oh, Jelly's *very* understanding,' he grins. 'Let's lock it in.'

'Tonight,' I tell him. 'I hear Sunflower Hotel has Friday night specials.'

'Let's call it a date then,' Jack says. 'A ridgy-didge one.'

I don't even try to hide my delight as I nod, childlike, his smile triggering a blip in a heart that has flatlined for far too long.

SOME DAYS ARE DIAMONDS

As the taxi pulls to a stop, Caroline Schaffer struggles to contain her inner White Rabbit. She's incredibly late. Late, late, late, and for a very, very, important date. The crowd milling on the footpath is not the only inconvenience Caroline has to plough through impatiently.

'Damn it!' The stuffy hotel foyer is awash with women and there's no parting the sea of grey hair and hormones standing between Caroline and the elevators. The fug of cheap perfume and lacquer leaves Caroline breathless. Or is the decision she hasn't yet made responsible for the tightening in her lungs and chest?

Another gaggle of women bursts into the foyer. All wear name badges pinned to their chests, and all bear the unmistakable bulge of money belts around middle-aged bellies. Some have peak caps perched on permed hair with words embroidered in big red letters: *Neil's Hot August Nanas.*

Damn you, Neil Diamond!

Surrounded and suffocating, Caroline has no choice but to fight her way through the lobby to reach a side exit. Ignoring the NO ENTRY—RESTORATION WORK IN PROGRESS sign and the accompanying construction and hard hat warning notices, she barges through the door and releases the breath she didn't know she'd been holding. The fresh air centres her and the cool, night-time breezes snap her mind back to the task at hand. With the courtyard dim and the garden beds mid-overhaul, therefore lacking the glitz of the hotel lobby, it feels and looks neglected, except for the pots of hedged foliage, clipped and tortured into such curious shapes that they no longer look like plants. Centrestage, snug against the building's exterior, sits *SkyPod*—the all-glass elevator: empty, lights on, doors open and taunting Caroline, daring her to board. She hesitates, glancing first at the time on her phone, then back into the crowded foyer. Inside are the only elevators Caroline has managed to ride without freaking out. They are spacious, fully enclosed, fast and she's had a very good reason to face her phobia these past few months. The love of a man who chooses a penthouse over a third-storey apartment. Rather than wait for the foyer to clear and risk being later still, she could let *SkyPod*—a relic of the past—deliver her to the fortieth floor and to her future.

If only she wasn't freaking out so much at the thought.

Skypod was built as a novelty elevator in the eighties; a reward for tourists en route to the *SkyLobby Cocktail Bar*, with its spectacular city views. The concept had excited a seven-year-old Caroline. But thirty-three years later, with the restaurant space turned into suites for visiting executives with business in the city, *SkyPod* takes tourists only as far as the Sky Lobby viewing level. Mainly for photo opportunities, an expensive cocktail, and for the thrill of creeping up the outside of a skyscraper in an all-glass cocoon; none of which interests Caroline. Access to floors higher than the Sky Lobby requires a change of elevator, secured with coded access only.

Luckily for Caroline, *SkyPod* entices fewer tourists these days and rarely at night. The contraption sits idle most of the time—unused by the harried and impatient professional person. The views are now mostly obscured, the building boxed in by two vista-blocking apartment towers side by side.

With one more check of the foyer, still bustling with concertgoers heading to the basement concert hall, Caroline takes a calming breath, steps into the glass bubble, presses the Sky Lobby button and closes her eyes in preparation for the terrifyingly slow ascent. Muttering the positivity mantra meant to control the sweaty palms and shortness of breath, she's waiting for the doors to close and for the creeping glass cocoon to begin its painstaking crawl, when a thud startles her. She opens her eyes wide just as a hand pokes between the doors, quickly followed by a man.

Caroline Schaffer is no longer alone.

'Whoa, just got that in time. Great minds, eh?' Big in stature, voice and presence, the new entrant has changed the small, cylindrical space she'd thought of as all hers into something now insufferably small. 'A bit crazy in that lobby,' the man gushes. 'Whoa!'

Conversation is the last thing Caroline wants or needs. She smiles in acknowledgement but concentrates her gaze on the changing floor numbers, counting each one off in her head.

First floor.

'Not going to the auditorium with everyone else?' the man asks.

'No.' *Second floor*, she counts.

'Not a Neil Diamond fan?' he persists.

'No.' *Third floor.*

'Whoa! Check out this view. Incredible, eh?'

Fourth floor. 'If you say so.'

'You know, with your eyes closed you are kinda missing it all?'

'That's the plan.' *Fifth floor, sixth floor, seventh, eighth ...*

Ninth floor, tenth floor. 'I can feel you staring at me,' she tells the stranger. 'Why?'

'Maybe the view inside is better than the one outside.'

Eleventh floor. 'Well, please stop.' *Twelfth floor.*

Barely ten seconds passes until she hears his voice again. 'She's a slow ride, don't you think? If it was a horse, I'd give it good kick to hurry her along. Since she's not,' he continues, 'and given we could be about to grow old together in this thing, we might get to know each other.'

Exasperation adds a dash of annoyance to Caroline's voice. 'I don't think so.'

'You don't think she's slow or—?'

'If you don't mind,' she cuts in, 'I'd rather not make elevator jokes. If you can't tell, I'm a little—'

'Oh, I can tell!' he quips. 'Figured conversation might help pass the time.'

The time! The trip is taking forever, and her forever might not wait. Gerald makes million-dollar deals between blinks and he'll be on a plane bound for Paris in an hour from now. If only she hadn't left all this until the last minute. But Caroline seems to have lost her decision-making ability; choosing this elevator is proof enough.

Might he assume she's not coming? If she dared look down to street level, would she see the concierge loading her future fiancé's bags, and the limousine speeding away from the hotel? Would a pang of regret or melancholy make him glance up and realise she's here and so determined to make the deadline, she's facing her greatest fear? Then the thought hit her. Did he even know about the aversion to elevators—or any of her pet hates and foibles? *Maybe not!*

'Hey, lady, you look like you could do with a seat, or a drink. Or both.'

'I'm not a lady. I'm Caroline.' His grin has Caroline regretting her chose of words. 'Please, don't worry about me. I'll be fine once I'm out of this contraption.'

'I'm not worrying. You're doing enough for the both of us.'

The man is moving around. Even with her eyes closed tight she can tell. She wishes he'd stop.

'You know, people designed this snazzy elevator to maximise the view. Have you tried opening your eyes and looking through your fingers? I do that in scary movies. It helps. Trust me.'

Caroline surprises herself when, through splayed fingers, she focuses on the interloper with the unusual twang to his voice. Starting at his feet, where well-worn boots poke out from under blue jeans, she notes his pale blue shirt hangs loose, but it's hitched where his fingers tuck into his pockets, exposing a brass belt buckle against a flat belly. She interrogates her own outfit, chosen specially for tonight: the *Franco D'mandi* with six-inch heels and a *sass & bide* pantsuit in Brisk Blueberry.

As her gaze connects with her companion's smiling face, the little cylindrical car shudders and bounces to a stop; the shock startles Caroline off her stillettos, and dire thoughts whirl around her head. *Oh God! I'm going to die in my D'mandis!*

Designed for a maximum of five passengers, the *SkyPod's* confined space leaves little room to fall; still a hand grasps her elbow and it's immediately comforting. Another jolt, another flicker of the car's dazzling halogen overhead lights and the once-creeping cocoon stills and falls dark.

'No, no, this can't be happening. Not to me. Not in here. Not tonight.' She hears the uncharacteristic hysterics in her voice. Like the late work meeting and the Uber driver with no sense of direction, the universe was trying to tell her something. 'It's a sign.'

'Nope,' the voice in the dark says flatly. 'It's a power outage.'

'But that's not possible.'

'I'm afraid it is,' he says. 'Open your eyes and see for yourself. The entire city is black. We're well and truly stuck.'

'Stuck? No, no,' she whines in a shrill voice she's unused to hearing.

What is going on? Caroline Schaffer does not whine or shriek. As corporate media advisor to a Fortune 500 company, she regularly holds court with the pushiest press pack. Even in the most sensitive boardroom settings, Caroline keeps her cool. But for some reason, no work scenario is as daunting as her current situation. 'I can't be stuck. I can't be. Someone's waiting for me.'

'You reckon you've got problems,' says the stranger. 'I've left my mother and twenty other small-town sexagenarians on the loose in the lobby.'

'That hardly sounds troublesome,' Caroline retorts.

'Ha! You haven't met my mother.' There's genuine love in the way his words trickle out on a laugh. 'Nor have you seen her Country Women's Association friends when they're frocked up. Not to mention revved up on bubbles and with front-row tickets to Neil

Diamond. On today's drive down, starting at dawn, I heard Myrtle Bertles ask if everyone remembered to bring a pair of clean underpants to toss on stage. The poor bloke won't know what's hit him —literally!'

While he seems amused by his own jokes, Caroline can't join in. Exasperation and fear has her close to tears. Although only half-listening, and in no mood for small talk, she concedes the stranger is right. The city stretching out before them, usually swathed in sparkly neon lights, is as black as pitch.

As trepidation gives way to total panic, she fumbles in the bag clasped in one hand and pulls out her iPhone.

'Damn! No connection and not much charge.'

'Who you planning to call?' he asks.

'The fire brigade, or building maintenance: security, someone, anyone. This is an emergency. I can't hang here. I have to get up to the fortieth floor.'

'Well, I hate to break the news, but in the event of a real emergency, elevators are programmed to go to ground. We won't go up. But, like I said, this isn't a fire or an evacuation. During a city-wide blackout the only thing to do is make the most of the view,' he says. 'Open your eyes. Enjoy the stars.'

'They are open,' Caroline says, 'and I can't see a thing, thank God.'

'Your pupils will need to adjust,' he tells her. 'Too much dazzling handsomeness at once will only add to your acrophobia. The name's Mackenzie—Mackenzie Pratt. Friends call me Mack. And you are Caroline, right? As in Neil Diamond's *Sweeeeeet Caroline—dah, dah, dah*. Nice to meet you.' When his hand connects with hers in the semi-dark, the firm hold again comforts. 'Geez, Caroline, you're really trembling.'

She snatches her hand back. 'I'll be fine once I'm on the fortieth floor. If only I'd waited my turn in the lobby with everyone else.'

'Why didn't you?' he asks.

'I didn't want to be late.'

'Look, I hate beginning a sentence with *Don't take this the wrong way*, but you are kind of uptight. Maybe if you tried relaxing.'

'I'm better alert and responsive than relaxed. It's what I'm used to.'

He huffs and Caroline imagines the accompanying smirk. 'That doesn't sound like much fun.'

'Corporate communications is not meant to be fun.' The rise in irritation makes her sound terser than intended and she's about to apologise for snapping when she detects a shrug—a ridiculous and inappropriate response from a man who's probably well into his forties. The temptation to lecture Mack Pratt on fun versus hard work, and the rewards awaiting the dedicated professional, came and went. A bloke from the bush is unlikely to want to listen or understand.

'Corporate communications must be a tough gig,' he says, finally breaking the silence. 'Are you good at it?'

What a strange question! 'Of course,' Caroline says.

She's worked hard to break through several glass ceilings until this glass ceiling. She lifts her face to the glass bubble serving as a roof and reminds herself how far she's come. Nothing makes a person work harder than a challenge, or the threat of having everything taken away. For that reason, no one is more driven than Caroline. Every goal has a strategy, every strategy an action, and every action has consequences.

Yes, it does! Caroline fiddles with the ring on her left hand. All week she'd twiddled the band in the hope a genie might appear and tell her what to do. A few times she'd even switched the diamond from one ring finger to the other, waiting for a sign. Even now the sparkling solitaire sits awkwardly, the fit a little sloppy, the design too flamboyant for her taste. *How many signs do you need, Caroline? The ring doesn't fit. What makes you think you'll fit any better into the Paris lifestyle?*

For one melancholy moment the flicker of emergency lighting throws up the faintest reflection of Caroline in *SkyPod*'s glass walls. Staring back is the little girl who'd survived the foster system. Expected to be mediocre at best, she showed the disbelievers how a child—even one who has lost all hope—can find the aptitude and confidence to change their life's direction. A career in management, one putting her in control of her destiny, had been Caroline's dream job. And she was there, finally, with the one person she'd made room for in her life waiting for her answer.

'Feeling bedazzled yet?' Mack asks.

'I beg your pardon?'

'The stars,' he explains. 'Ten times more glittery than a city's neon lights.'

'I suppose, but to be honest, Mack, I'm only looking up to stop me looking down.'

'Speaking of dazzling…' He inches closer until she can see the features in his face and gives her arm a nudge. 'Even in the moonlight, I can see you haven't stopped twirling that not-to-be-missed diamond solitaire you've got on your left hand. Makes me wonder if it should be there at all.'

Caroline stuffs the ring in a pocket of her trousers. 'It's new.' She wants to be mad at his impertinence, but a trace of amusement loosens his lips and widens his grin into a toothy smile. 'What's with the goofy grin?'

'Your reaction when I mentioned the bling. Don't worry. I'm not about to rob you. I have all the diamonds I need.'

'Oh, really?' Caroline immediately regrets her haughty retort; not that he seems bothered.

'Yep! The biggest diamond in the universe is right up there and it's mine whenever I want it.'

She laughs for the first time; what a shame it's such a condescending one. 'You're referring to the stars?'

'Not just any stars,' he replies. 'The Southern Cross is the best-known constellation in the southern hemisphere; easily recognisable by the cross-shaped asterism formed by its five bright stars. And there,' he points, 'is the white dwarf star of the constellation, Centaurus. Unfortunately, a layer of hydrogen and helium gases keeps the three thousand kilometre-wide core of crystallised carbon hidden. All that aside, however, coming in at 2.27 thousand trillion trillion tonnes, it's definitely the mother of all diamonds. I mean, we're talking 10 billion trillion trillion carats—or a one followed by thirty-four zeros.'

'Thank you for the clarification,' Caroline quips.

'And do you know the best thing about a sky diamond?' he continues as if she hadn't spoken.

'No, but I'm sure you'll tell me.'

'Since you asked,' he says. 'Sky diamonds come with no promises, no strings attached, and no demands. They want nothing from us but admiration. No decisions needed whatsoever.'

Ignoring the no-strings comment, Caroline manages a smile. 'You want me to concur there's a diamond in the sky? Next you'll be suggesting there's a Lucy in the sky with diamonds.'

'You're a Beatles fan?' he asks.

'No, not particularly, but people used to think the song title was code for LSD.'

'No doubt about us humans!' Mack says. 'We can tell ourselves anything is correct and go around convincing others we're right, in the same way people were convinced the earth was flat. But did you know those early explorers all used one thing to navigate their way around the world? The stars!' he says. 'I use the very same ones to help me navigate through life.'

The stiffness in Caroline's straight back softens, as does her tone and the flinty demeanor she blames on a lifelong fear. 'I'm intrigued,' she admits. 'How do stars help?'

'Simple, really,' Mack replies. 'When I feel overwhelmed, I go bush. Nothing frees the mind more effectively than a night camping. You haven't lived until you've slept in a swag sandwiched between mineral-rich earth and a star-studded sky. Different to a penthouse and four-poster bed, admittedly,' he remarks. 'Not that I've tried one of those. Congratulations on your engagement, by the way. Do you mind if I ask a question?'

Caroline cocks her head to the side. 'Do I have a choice?'

'Well, it's just, you're newly engaged, and with a beaut bit of bling, which makes me wonder ...' He hesitates, but briefly. 'What I'm trying to say is, I've seen crows on roadkill look more excited than you.'

Convivial Caroline snaps back to cold as she retorts. 'Perhaps my lack of excitement, Mr Pratt, is to do with being stuck on the outside of a building in a see-through barnacle with a stranger interrogating me.'

'Hmm, when you put it that way, it doesn't sound too good.'

As silence stretches between them, Caroline regrets her rudeness. Imagine if he hadn't joined her in the lift and his annoying chatter wasn't keeping her mind occupied? The man *is* funny and knowledge-able and a wonderful conversationalist, and while she can't see him well, his voice is kind and modulated, his words measured.

'I'm sorry. I don't mean to be rude. I'm a little on edge.'

'I get there's something big going on and I want to say, whether it's the acrophobia or the ring thing, I'm a good listener. Talking might take your mind off whatever's worrying you.'

'No, thanks,' she says until another small shudder rattles both the pod and her poise. 'Oh, no!' She grabs for the metal handrail and gushes. 'I'm going to die. He's waiting for me. On the fortieth floor. I'm supposed to tell him my answer before he flies out tonight, but instead I'm going to fall to my death and life will end just when it's about to be amazing.'

'Hey, come on. No one is dying.' He takes her hand in his, holding firm, squeezing tight. 'Keep talking. Tell me about this bloke in the penthouse. I'm guessing he had a special way of popping the question, eh? Did he hire a fancy restaurant for the two of you? Charter a private yacht? Hold a big bash in the penthouse?'

'Oh, no, Gerald's a very private person,' she hears herself say. 'It was in his apartment, one night after work last week.'

'I see, so, if you don't mind me asking, why is it you didn't give him your answer when he gave you the ring?'

'I, ah, needed time.'

'Ouch!' Mack flicks his hand and pretends to suck on a sore finger.

'What?' she demands. 'What's that response supposed to mean?'

He stops sucking his finger and, trapping the hand close to his armpit, feigns more pain. 'If the girl I was proposing to said she needed time, I reckon I'd pretty much have her answer right there.'

'Oh really?' Caroline challenged. 'Then I guess you've never asked a girl, because choices are not always clear-cut.'

'Clear-cut?' He scoffs. 'I'll have you know I did ask, and she said yes on the spot.'

When the words *lucky her* are the first thing to enter Caroline's head, she bats them away. Then, for reasons she doesn't understand, she bristles, her eyes narrowing. 'A small town is not exactly Paris,' she says, 'and I imagine your wife had to do little more than move across town from her childhood ranch to yours. Saying "yes" is easy when the stakes are not high.'

His head tilts to the side. 'Country Australia doesn't have ranches any more than we have penthouses,' he retorts. 'We have farmhouses, homesteads, or stations—or just plain properties, and every farmer or grazier contributes to the Australia's food bowl. Try living without us.'

'Well,' she said combatively, feeling well and truly put in her place. 'Wherever you come from—'

'Sunflower,' he butts in.

Caroline is bemused. 'The town you come from is called Sunflower? Oh, never mind!' She flaps a dismissive hand, her patience waning. 'I'm simply suggesting there's no comparison between toting a suitcase to the other side of a country town and packing up one's life to relocate overseas and start over in a brand new country.'

Caroline pauses to replay her words: *start over*. Was fear of starting over her problem? Hardly surprising, given her childhood. Giving up her life in Australia will mean giving up her home and …

'I can't.' Her cheeks burn with both embarrassment and the tears of a child uprooted too many times. 'I love my little ground floor flat. It's no penthouse, but it's safe and it's mine, and no one can ever, *ever* rip me out of my home again. Never, never again. Oh, good grief! Look at me crying over nothing. I'm a mess.'

'I am looking at you.' He grins. 'And you're not a mess, but you are intriguing. Tell me how a child can be ripped away from her home?'

'Homes—plural,' she tells him. 'Foster homes.' She straightens her spine and forces a smile. 'But I showed everyone. And now, finally, a penthouse in Paris!'

'You speak as if you've won a prize,' Mack says.

She looks at her companion—what she can make out now her eyes have adapted to the darkness—and all sensibilities escape her and drift into the night sky. Caroline should know better than to reveal her weakness—her past—and to a complete stranger, no less. She *should* focus on getting out of this death pod and on with her life. *And, yes, go to Paris, Caroline. Why not?*

This Mack fellow can no more understand her hardship than she can fathom his small-town existence and country roots than run deep. Caroline had none, and everyone knows what happens to a plant with no roots.

When Caroline had been a child, support and counselling for wards of the state had lacked empathy and follow-through. No one cared how many times she ran away, or how many nights she slept on borrowed sofas. By day, she'd begged on street corners and outside cafes. Never for money, though. Only jobs or work experience opportunities. When others gave up on her, she'd worked hard, studied harder, and succeeded. She's made something of herself, by herself. Surely that makes her worthy of a prize?

'If you were to ask me,' Mack's voice captures her attention, 'whoever is waiting on the fortieth floor is the prize winner.'

'Gerald doesn't expect me to prove myself. He tells me I'm not expected to work,' she says. Then asks, 'But what would I do? I don't even speak the language.'

'You'll be in Paris, the city of *luuuuurve!*' He clasps both hands over his heart, his grin cocky. 'And Paris is the place for lovers. I should know; I met my wife there.'

Wife, yes! Why did disappointment dent Caroline's good mood and drag her shoulders back down? 'Tell me about her, Mack.'

'We grew up less than an hour's drive away from each other and met on an almost-empty school bus, but I had to wait until I saw her in a crowded Paris nightclub to make a move. Ah, *Pah-ree!* What a place,' he says dreamily. 'Irises overflowing in the Jardin du Luxembourg, the afternoon light on the Seine, cobbled streets crowded until the early hours of the morning. Gotta love a place where the entire city seems to come out at night to sit at tables on the street or cram into packed cafes. The only thing missing on those nights were stars. Too much pollution.'

'You're very familiar with Paris.'

'As much as any twenty-year-old on a thirty-day Contiki Tour of Europe. My mother was keen for me to get the travel bug out of my system early. Less keen on me marrying before my twenty-first. But it was love at first sight, that night.'

And married after six weeks! Caroline muses. She's about to notch up six months with a man and here she is, twenty-odd floors away, still undecided after a week of wondering.

'I brought Deb back home to the family and they fell in love with her, too.'

'You were lucky to have a home and a family.'

'You have a home,' Mack says.

'With mortgage payments I can't meet if I give up my job.' She stopped for a few seconds. 'You know, the thought of selling my one piece of independence—my home—terrifies me.'

'So, your indecision is not about loving enough, it's about leaving the place you feel safest.'

'Wow!' She gushes as tears swirl in her eyes and tip over onto both cheeks. 'And here's you thinking Neil Diamond with his knicker-throwing nanas is the luckiest guy tonight. Aren't you thrilled you stepped inside this elevator with me?'

'Actually—' Mack begins, but a scream roars up Caroline's throat as the pod shudders and falls several floors, enough to drop her stomach.

She grabs Mack with both arms, burrowing her nails into his shoulders and burying her face into his chest, eyes squeezed tight. 'Oh my God! This is it; the reason there's been no sign after a week's worth of *will I or won't I.* My life ends here, tonight. No decision necessary. Instead, I'll plummet to my death knowing the last thing I did on this earth was insult a sweet stranger because he happened to hit a raw nerve or two. 'By the way.' She pulls back to look at Mack. 'You were so right when you said—'

'Shh!' he presses the tips of four fingers to her lips. 'For goodness' sake, stop speaking, Caroline, and let me hold you.' His lips are warm on her ear. 'You're not alone. I'm here. Hold tight and breath with me.'

As he draws in a deliberately loud breath, she's aware of two powerful hands wrapping around the small of her back, and two hearts pressing together, pounding in sync. Tightly he holds her and tighter she holds him back.

'Talk to me, Mack, please. Tell me something, anything.'

Without hesitation, Mack Pratt serenades Caroline with small talk about the stars and a moon that shines like fairy lights in the sky above the small town of Sunflower.

When the pod's full complement of halogen lights flicker on, Caroline reluctantly breaks the embrace, straightens her frame and sucks some brightness into her voice.

'Well, I sure picked the right guy to get stuck with in a tight space.'

She has no idea how long they'd held on, other than it was long enough to have their body heat iron deep creases into Mack's shirt. Caroline is straightening her own clothes and fussing with her hair when Mack flashes a cheeky grin, with duelling dimples she hadn't seen in the dark adding a childish charm to his jaw with its masculine shadow beard.

'I reckon we dropped a few floors,' Mack says. 'Totally the wrong direction for you, I'm afraid.'

'I no longer care if we go down rather than up,' she tells him. 'As long as that drop doesn't happen too many more times.'

'Aw, I dunno, Caroline, I kind of enjoy a good cuddle.'

Awkward and a little self-conscious, she pokes her wayward brown strand of hair back into the bun at the nape of her neck, and plucks at the collar of her white linen shirt to let air circulate.

'Tell me more about Sunflower, Mack.'

'Let's get comfortable first.'

After settling on the pod's carpeted floor, he draws one knee up to drape a toned forearm on top. The man is so unruffled, so casual and so country, Caroline waits for him to whip out a sprig of wheat to chew. But stereotyping is wrong, as is pigeonholing him as a bushy. Mack Pratt is far from typical.

'The locals will tell you Sunflower is smack-bang in the middle of somewhere.'

'Um, the actual saying is *middle of nowhere*.'

'No,' he corrects. 'Sunflower might be a crumb-on-a-map country town and not a sunflower field in sight, but it's somewhere all right. A couple of hours short of Clarkesville, a few hours long of Ugly Joe's Creek and a little way to the left. And that puts us smack-bang in the middle of—'

'Somewhere. I get it. Cute!' Caroline says.

'Thanks,' he grins. 'How about you park it here with me. Sit and look up rather than down. The view's amazing.' When he pats the floor, Caroline settles next to him and together they stare up through the glass ceiling. 'Few things will get me back to the city in the middle of winter,' he tells her, 'My mother and her cohorts roped me into driving them.'

'You're not worried about your mother in a blackout?'

'Nah, wherever they are, they'll be warm. In the bus, twenty-six sexagenarians together were a hormone-powered heater.'

Caroline laughs. 'You caught a bus?'

'I drove the bus.'

'You're a bus driver?' she exclaims.

'Not hard to end up a Jack-of-all-trades when you grow up in a small town. I also have a reputation as the town's soft touch,' he says proudly. 'The ladies needed a lift. I volunteered.'

'Are you an only child?' she asks.

'Four kids in total. Two boys and two girls, but I'm the good one; the one Mum relies on. Ask and she'll tell you.' Mack laughs. 'She left her camera in the room and I figured this bubble might get me up and back while they queued—first for nervous wees, then for the Convention Centre elevators.'

'You are aware *SkyPod* is an express service? Not express as in fast —obviously,' Caroline explains. 'Express as in no stops. Anyone can take this elevator direct to the *SkyLobby*, but the penthouse suites need a code.'

'I'm acutely aware of the express facility now and feel a little silly.' He smiles, shrugs. 'But also happy with my decision. The view turned out to be not too shabby and I do feel at peace under the stars. Ten years ago, they helped me make one of the biggest decisions of my life.'

'Oh? Can I ask what the decision was?'

'To give the country away and try my luck in the big smoke,' he says. 'And after agonising about the decision for months, I'll tell you what I learned. City or country, it's the same blanket of stars, only we see more of them in the outback because there's no light pollution.'

'We have light pollution in the city?'

'Loads! Artificial light comes from all your neons and streetlights blotting out the night stars,' he explains. 'I'm part way through an application to have Sunflower designated an official D–S–P—Dark Sky Place. They call them "pristine dark skies",' he says, as if reading Caroline's bemused expression. 'With the glare from artificial light minimised if we regulate buildings and infrastructure, we can fully enjoy the night sky. Developing and promoting dark sky places … well, we can hope future generations look away from the glow of their electronic devices and know the joy of camping out, finding the man in the moon, and wishing on stars.' Mack pauses, blued by the moonlight, his mien equally blue.

'What?' Caroline asks, taking his hand in hers.

'One day Dad said to me, "Mackenzie, I love you so much I'd paint the moon to prove it". For years I'd look up and wish he would. I remember my first red moon. I told everyone at school, "My dad painted that".'

'What a beautiful story. Your father sounds special.'

'Yeah, he's my greatest inspiration. Taught me to love the planet.'

'It might surprise you to know I used to sit outside a lot at night. After they removed me from my birth mother, I would wish for a family of my own. Now here we are all grown up. When did that happen, Mack? When did we stop seeing stars as something magical, capable of making dreams come true?'

'Clearly, I'm yet to grow up,' he responds. 'There are things I still wish for.'

'Like?' she asks.

Without missing a beat, Mack says, 'More of what I have in Sunflower. As much as I appreciated the overseas travel opportunities, and I'm grateful for Paris, there is something spectacular about the southern sky.'

Ah, yes, Paris! Caroline muses. *Love at first sight, wife at home. Grow up and get real, Caroline!*

'I'm assuming, Mack, your Paris proposal was something super romantic? A table for two in one of those cafes you mentioned? Under the Arc de Triomphe, perhaps?'

Mack snorts a laugh. 'No way! I waited until we got to Sunflower. I wanted Deb to get accustomed to the family. With my siblings breeding like rabbits, there could be as many as a dozen clamouring for talk time at once. We're family, but we're not for the faint-hearted. When we get together, we're loud and excitable and in each other's faces. We are also the type to interfere in each other's lives. No better way to show Deb what makes me than proposing during a Sunday barbeque with the family to share in the occasion.'

Caroline's jaw dropped. 'You proposed marriage in the backyard and in front of the entire family?'

Mack sat back, his eyes narrowed. 'Something funny?'

'Oh, no, on the contrary,' she replies. 'It sounds amazing.' *Perfect, in fact!* 'And you've left your wife behind in Sunflower tonight? She's not into Neil Diamond?'

'Deb's not into me,' Mack says with a rueful smile. 'Unlike the rest of the family's unions, my marriage was brief. When we were in Europe, we'd discussed the places we might put down roots. And, we returned to Australia with little money between us so we ended up staying. As far as I'm concerned, the best is often right under our nose, but we don't notice because of the clutter and confusion.'

'Like we don't see a night sky in the city, you mean?'

'Yeah.' He nods. 'Only Deb didn't agree. She stayed in Sunflower long enough to rack up a debt the size of a small European country. These days she's living in the light-pollution capital of Australia with her even shinier Smeg appliances, a new husband, and my son.'

Caroline senses a change, the joker's smile less genuine. 'You have a son?'

'Oh yes. Jaxon. I see him regularly enough, and I've no doubt he'll come home to the country in time. He definitely has country-loving genes, like his dad. His favourite outfit is a cowboy hat and chaps. He's even demanding a pony for his tenth birthday.'

'What kid doesn't dream of a horse? I did,' Caroline confesses.

'Well, guess what? I have five—Paddy, Lacy, Clancy, Wilbur and Barney, the foal. Plus, I'm father to two retired working dogs aptly named: Comehere and Dammit, who'll be giving birth any day. I have my hands full.'

'I'm not sure I'd trust myself to raise anything. Years ago I adopted two lazy cats. They ran away.'

'Does you-know-who,' he thumbs north, 'have any kids? Is that your dilemma? Are you worried you'll be a stepmum?'

'Good grief, no! His daughter is close to my age.'

'Then what is it about yourself you don't trust?' Mack asks. 'Whatever happened to you as a kid in the foster system doesn't make you any less capable. Kids can realise their full potential, despite a fragile start. You're proof.'

'And you're nice,' she says.

'Thank you,' he replies. 'That's Awkward Moment number 2 out of the way.'

'You're counting our moments?' she chuckles.

He grins. 'I'm certainly enjoying them.'

'Okay, so what next, Mack Pratt?'

'Well, that depends on what your answer will be to Mr Fortieth Floor?'

The flat feeling returns as Caroline drags the ring out of her pocket, placing it on her palm. Not hesitating when Mack takes the diamond between his thumb and finger, she watches him twist and turn the stone to catch the lights. But it's when he hands the ring back that his words cause her breath to catch.

'Will you, Caroline?' he asks.

'I, um, ah … Will I what, Mack?'

'Will you marry *him*? Up there.'

Looking at the ring in her palm she says, 'This is one of those diamonds a girl only gets one shot at in her life and it's dazzled me into believing I want something I've never wanted before. While half an hour ago I was in a rush to reach him, I'm suddenly incapable of deciding. All week I've been expecting a sign. I can only guess it's *Skypod*.'

'Which means what?' Mack asks.

'Well, when the elevator finally moves, if it goes up I guess it is meant to be.'

As if on cue, the stars disappear, outshone by halogen down lights firing to life around the *SkyPod's* perimeter. The pair scramble to their feet as the glass barnacle bounces up and down a few times. With hands locked together, breaths held, and eyes fixed on each other, Mack smiles.

'Well, sweet Caroline, it seems the elevator is experiencing the same trouble deciding. But, if it *does* go up …' His hands tighten. 'I'll remain forever grateful to *Skypod* and glad I met you tonight.'

The tingle in Caroline's stomach has nothing to do with the pitching elevator and everything to do with the earnest blue eyes staring at her from under a bedraggled black fringe. 'And if it's down, Mack?'

'If it's down?' he repeated. 'Remember, there's a nice little place in the middle of somewhere with its own patch of clear sky and as many diamonds as you could want. Maybe you might—'

'Yes!' She hisses the word as the elevator starts its slow descent.

'Is that answer a "Yes, you'll definitely come", Caroline, or are you saying that in the moment. And while you'll try to make it out that way one day, you'll end up stuck somewhere halfway with some really annoying bloke who changes your mind and turns you around?'

'Oh, Mack, I promise I'm not usually such a mess. Tonight has been so overwhelming and I'm late and ... I'm so sorry.'

'Well, if you ever fancy a small trip and a tree change, consider Sunflower. Here!' He fishes a business card out of his wallet. 'You'll have the biggest diamond in the universe, and a job if you want one.'

She reads the card. 'Managing Editor?'

'Ever since the media company mothership set us loose to save a buck I'm it: Managing Editor, Editor, Layout, Classifieds, Ad Sales. Regional towns need their local rag. So, like I said, Jack-of-all-trades, which means I can pretty much guarantee if you apply for a job with *The Sunflower Tribune* you'll get the position, including part-time bus driver on your days off.' His smile is cautious.

'Thank you, Mack.' She's businesslike again, slipping her coat on in anticipation of the cold. 'While you make county life appealing, I, umm—'

'Yes, Paris!' He sounds defeatist for the first time all night until the doors open and he's free to leave. 'Good luck with Paris, sweet Caroline.'

'Yoo-hoo! Mackenzie, honey, I'm here!' From amidst the mob that's spilled into the courtyard to wait out the blackout, a woman is waving a peak cap in the air, her voice shrill over the rhubarb of an anxious crowd. 'Are you okay, sweetheart? Did you get my camera?'

Mack waves an arm over the mayhem of milling hotel evacuees as he weaves through a small gap to join his mother. 'I've never been better,' he calls back, taking a last look at Caroline as she passes by. 'I've spent the last hour making a new friend. Here she is.' His hand on Caroline's elbow stops her dead and she stares into the same beautiful, blue eyes. Mack has his mother's face.

'Oh, hello dear, don't you look smart. Lovely suit,' the woman says, and Caroline sees where Mack gets his warmth and his smile. 'What do you call the colour?'

'Um, Brisk Blueberry.'

'Well, I hate to be brisk Betty.' She chuckles, her wit and her wink so much like her son's. 'They're letting us back in soon and we wanted a group photo while we all still have our knickers. See?' As she waves her pink panties in the air, Caroline can see the woman's cohorts following suit.

'Steady on, ladies,' Mack says, chuckling. 'Here, take my phone, Mum. You know how the camera works, right?'

'Yes, but—'

'Okay, go on, get the girls ready and I'll take the shot myself, after I try a shot at something else.' He turns to Caroline, kissing her hard on the mouth. '*Au revoir*, Caroline. I trust you will make the right decision for you. Trust yourself to do the same, okay? And if it ends up being Paris, then at least we'll always have *SkyPod*,' he says with a wink. 'Here's looking at you, kid.'

Sunflower Tribune headline: One Friday, three months later …
Pristine Dark Sky Application Underway.

Classifieds/Public Notices: One Friday, six months later …
It's with the greatest pleasure that Mr and Mrs Pratt welcome Caroline Schaffer, formerly of 'somewhere else', into the family.

Classifieds/Births Notices: One Friday, nine months later …
Baby boy born to Mack and Caroline Pratt. They've named him Neil.

THE END (or is it?)

IF YOU ENJOYED MY BIG LITTLE TALES …

Have you read my full-length fiction, including my #5 bestselling debut Australian novel, *House for all Seasons*? (See next page) Do you like to review books on Goodreads or post to Facebook and Instagram? If you have friends that aren't into books—weird, right?—what better way to introduce them to the joy of fiction than recommending short stories easily read over a cuppa or on their daily commute. NB: **The *Country Cush* collection** is available as two ebooks: *That Time in Tanglewood* and *One Friday in Sunflower*.

Find these and all my novels online. Or come to www.jennjmcleod.com and let me know your favourite *Country Crush* story; one day I might make it into a big one.

Finally, if you haven't already, check out **Pilyara Press.** I am blessed to have the support of an awesome bunch of women writers and publishing experts and so grateful to Shelley Kenigsberg and Desney King for their editing expertise. Thank you, Jennifer Scoullar and Pilyara Press, for the butt-kick I needed to get this book done. **For more fab fiction: www.pilyarapress.com**

HOUSE FOR ALL SEASONS – A Calingarry Crossing novel

The 2013 #5 bestselling Australian debut novel.

Four women, four lives unravelled. The truth will bind them forever.

Bequeathed a century-old house, four estranged friends return to their hometown, Calingarry Crossing, where each must stay for a season at the Dandelion House to fulfil the wishes of their benefactor, Gypsy. But coming home to the country stirs shameful memories of the past for all four, including the tragic end-of-school muck-up-day accident twenty years earlier.

Sara—a breast cancer survivor afraid to fall in love;

Poppy—an ambitious journo still craving her father's approval;

Amber—spoilt and addicted to pills and cosmetic procedures;

Caitlin—a doctor frustrated by her flat-lining life.

At Dandelion House, the women will discover something about themselves as well as a secret tying all four to each other and to the house forever.

For more info: **books2read.com/HouseForAllSeasons**

SIMMERING SEASON – A Calingarry Crossing novel

A country hotel, an unexpected house guest, and a school reunion. Maggie's perfect storm is about to lift the lid off a lifetime of secrets.

Dan Ireland, a work-weary police crash investigator still hell-bent on punishing himself for his misspent youth, has ample reason for not going home to Calingarry Crossing for the school reunion, but one very good reason why he should—Maggie Lindeman.

Maggie is back in Calingarry Crossing trying to sell the family pub, while also dealing with a restless seventeen-year-old son, a father with dementia, a fame-obsessed musician husband back in the city, and a dwindling bank account.

The last thing she needs is a surprise house guest for the summer.

Fiona Bailey-Blair, daughter of an old friend and spoilt with everything but the truth, whips up a maelstrom of gossip when she blows into town in search of answers.

This storm season, as Maggie's past and present converge with the unexpected, she'll discover … *there's no keeping a lid on some secrets.*

(First published by Simon & Schuster, *Simmering Season* is another Calingarry Crossing novel from the author of *House of Wishes* and the bestselling *House for all Seasons.*)

For more info: **books2read.com/Simmering-Season**

Also available in audio with bonus song track: Aurora/Ulverscroft

HOUSE OF WISHES – A Calingarry Crossing novel

Three wishes, three mothers, three generations:

Dandelion House is ready to reveal its secrets.

Dandelion House, 1974

Two teenage girls—strangers—make a pact to keep a secret.

Calingarry Crossing, 2014

For forty years, Beth and her mum have been everything to each other, but Beth is blindsided when her mother dies, and her last wish is to have her ashes spread in a small-town cemetery.

On the outskirts of Calingarry Crossing, when Beth comes across a place called Dandelion House Retreat, her first thought is how appealing the name sounds. With her stage career waning, and struggling to see a future without her mum, her marriage, and her child, she hopes it's a place where she can begin to heal.

After meeting Tom, a local cattleman, Beth is intrigued by his stories of the cursed, century-old river house and its reclusive owner, Gypsy. The more Beth learns, however, the more she questions her mother's wishes.

When meeting Beth leads Tom to uncover a disturbing connection to the old house, he must decide if the truth will help a grieving daughter or hurt her more.

Or should Dandelion House keep its last, long-held secret?

For more info: **books2read.com/House-of-wishes**

Also available in audio: Download or ask your library.

SEASON OF SHADOW AND LIGHT

Sometime this season ... the secret keeper must tell, the betrayed must trust, the hurt must heal.

When it seems everything Paige trusts is beginning to betray her, she leaves her husband at home and sets off on a road trip with six-year-old Matilda and Nana Alice in tow.

Stranded amid rising floodwaters, on a detour taking them to the tiny town of Coolabah Tree Gully, Paige discovers the greatest betrayal of all happened there twenty years earlier.

Someone knows that truth can wash away the darkest shadows, but ...

are some secrets best kept for the sake of others?

For more info: **books2read.com/SeasonOfShadowAndLight**

THE OTHER SIDE OF THE SEASON

There's another side to every story.

When offering to drive her brother to Byron Bay to escape the bitter Blue Mountains' winter, Sidney neglects to mention her planned detour to the small seaside town of Watercolour Cove.

Thirty-five years earlier, Watercolour Cove is a very different place. Two brothers are working the steep, snake-infested slopes of a Coffs Coast banana plantation. Seventeen-year-old David does his share, but the budding artist spends too much time daydreaming about becoming the next Pro Hart and skiving off with the teasing and tantalisingly pretty Tilly from the neighbouring property.

Life is simple on top of the mountain for Tilly, David, and his older brother, Matthew, until the winter of 1979 when tragedy strikes, starting a chain reaction which will ruin lives for years to come. Those who can, escape the Greenhill plantation. One stays—trapped on the mountain, and haunted by memories and lost dreams.

That is until the arrival of a curious young woman, named Sidney, whose love of family shows everyone …

The truth can heal, what's wrong can be righted, the lost can be found and there's another side to every story.

For more info: **books2read.com/TheOtherSideOfTheSeason**

A PLACE TO REMEMBER

A portrait, an obsession, a curious daughter, and an affair to remember.

Running away for the second time in her life, twenty-seven-year-old Ava believes the cook's job at a country B&B is perfect until she meets the owner's son, John Tate. The young fifth-generation grazier is a beguiling blend of both man and boy, and a terrible flirt. With their connection immediate and intense, they begin a clandestine affair right under the noses of John's formidable parents.

Thirty years later, Ava returns to Candlebark Creek with Tina, a daughter determined to meet her mother's lost love for herself. While struggling to find her own place in the world, Tina discovers an urban myth about a love-struck man, a forgotten engagement ring, and a dinner reservation back in the eighties. Now she must decide if revealing the truth will hurt more than it heals.

For more info: **books2read.com/APlaceToRemember**

Also available in audio: Download or ask your library.